BOOK THREE

Vampire

BOUND

Other books by R. A. Steffan

The Last Vampire: Book One
The Last Vampire: Book Two
The Last Vampire: Book Three
The Last Vampire: Book Four
The Last Vampire: Book Five
The Last Vampire: Book Six

Circle of Blood: Book One
Circle of Blood: Book Two
Circle of Blood: Book Three
Circle of Blood: Book Four
Circle of Blood: Book Five
Circle of Blood: Book Six

(with Jaelynn Woolf)

The Complete Horse Mistress Collection

The Complete Lion Mistress Collection

The Complete Dragon Mistress Collection

Antidote: Love and War, Book 1
Antigen: Love and War, Book 2
Antibody: Love and War, Book 3
Anthelion: Love and War, Book 4
Antagonist: Love and War, Book 5

BOOK THREE

BOUND

R. A. STEFFAN

Vampire Bound: Book Three

For information, contact the author at
http://www.rasteffan.com/contact/

Cover art by Deranged Doctor Design

First Edition: September 2020

Author's Note

This book contains adult material. It is intended for a mature audience.

Table of Contents

ONE

Zorah Bright was as pissed off as I'd ever seen her. I hugged myself as I watched her pacing around Leonides' living room, her eyes flashing with an unnatural copper glow. Fortunately or unfortunately, I was too overwhelmed with what I'd recently learned about the Fae's plans to take over Earth to really appreciate the full glory of my friend in a rampaging temper.

In many ways, Zorah and I had been cut from similar cloth when we'd known each other as casual friends and coworkers. We were both beaten down, living near the poverty level, and self-sufficient by necessity. The world of low-wage service industry work had no place for women with an attitude. You smiled, you played nice no matter how much shit was thrown in your face, and you reminded yourself over and over that other people — the customer, your boss, the bill collector on the phone — were always right.

Apparently, becoming a vampire could be a liberating experience.

"I can't *believe* you two idiots would do something so... so... *idiotic*! What the *hell* were you thinking, going to *Dhuinne* of all places? *You could've been killed!*"

I'd decided the moment I saw Zorah's thunderous expression to let Leonides take point on the rebuttal. The way I saw things, I was doing pretty well simply by virtue of not being huddled on the floor, rocking back and forth in a corner.

By contrast, Ransley Thorpe—Zorah's English vampire lover—appeared calm and collected as she raged. Arms crossed loosely in front of him, he surveyed the motley group scattered around the living room with incisive blue eyes.

"I'm not sure you're allowed to get stroppy over this one, love," he observed in a mild tone. "At least Vonnie didn't barge into Dhuinne *alone*."

I'd already heard the cliff-notes version of the escapade he was referring to, if not the full story. Still, I knew enough to be aware that Zorah had once snuck into Dhuinne without telling anyone in an attempt to save her father, and nearly died before Rans showed up to rescue her. The near-fatal expedition was still a sore point between them. That much became obvious when Zorah whirled on Rans, glaring.

"*I wasn't alone,*" Zorah said through gritted teeth. She stabbed a finger toward the injured Fae sitting on the other side of the room, his spare frame draped over an armchair as though it were a throne. "*He* was with me—as you know perfectly well."

Albigard, the injured Fae in question, looked more bored by the exchange than anything else.

Rans followed her gesture and raised a slow eyebrow. "Oh, yes—sorry. Let me rephrase that. At least Vonnie didn't barge into Dhuinne with only a *backstabbing Fae arsehole* in tow."

Albigard made a show of examining his fingernails. "When I stab you, vampire, it won't be in the back."

Leonides, who had claimed a spot near the door leading to the interior hallway, squeezed the bridge of his nose and rubbed at the corners of his eyes.

"If we could circle back to the point...?" he prompted. "Vonnie went to Dhuinne to find information about her missing son. I went to Dhuinne to help her, and to find out what happened to Albigard. We both got some of the answers to our questions. Unfortunately, none of those answers are what you'd call *good*."

Rans and Albigard didn't stop eyeing each other like a pair of tomcats staking out territory, but Zorah threw up her hands in defeat before collapsing into a chair with a gusty sigh.

"Okay, yes, fine," she said. "Albigard—you look like shit, and that's not a look I'm used to seeing on you. What happened?"

The Fae didn't break expression. "As expected, I was punished for killing the one responsible for the death of my brother and sister. Next question?"

I shivered. "They were torturing him, Zorah," I clarified, trying not to think about iron spikes embedded in skin... of thorns impaling naked flesh.

Leonides' expression settled into grim lines. "They had him staked out in front of the Court like some kind of bad performance art. Iron spikes, crucifixion... the whole deal. Our original plan had been to get into Dhuinne, get whatever information we could, and head straight back to Earth. Unfortunately, that plan went out the window after your cat-*sidhe* friend led us right past Albigard on our way out."

Both Zorah and Rans looked surprised.

"The cat-*sidhe* was involved?" Rans asked. "That's... interesting."

"It seemed deliberate," I offered. "We were smuggled in through the back door of the Court building when we arrived, allegedly so our presence wouldn't upset the populace. But afterward, we came out of the main entrance in broad daylight like it was no big deal. Then we saw Albigard, and when we freaked out, the cat disappeared like a ghost—right before the you-know-what hit the fan."

"I get the impression that relations between the Seelie and Unseelie aren't all roses and rainbows these days," Leonides said. "And normally, I wouldn't give two shits about Fae politics. But..."

He gestured wearily toward Albigard, prompting him to speak.

"The Unseelie are plotting to install a ruling class of magical humans on Earth, in preparation for moving the Fae Court to this world from Dhuinne," he said, the words toneless.

There was a beat of absolute silence.

"Say that again," Rans said.

"Are your ears defective, bloodsucker? You heard me the first time," the Fae replied.

"Is this because of the crazy, out-of-control plant life on Dhuinne taking everything over?"

Zorah asked quietly. "Is that why they're trying to find a new world?"

"The Fae realm's magic is out of balance," Albigard said. "The Seelie would prefer to seek out the root cause in hopes of fixing it, but the Unseelie have... other ideas."

"And all of this is presumably why Nigellus has been harping on and on about the missing human kids," Leonides put in. "All the stuff he's been saying about how it would be everyone's problem before long? Well, he was right. Now it's definitely everyone's problem."

I scrubbed at my face, knowing there was really no choice other than to face this situation head-on—even if I'd much rather run away screaming and hide in a closet for the next few months.

"So... can the Fae seriously do this?" I asked. "I mean, on the surface, the whole thing sounds completely crazy. Are they actually powerful enough to crush human civilization with magic, and just... what? Move in and take over?"

"Yes," Albigard said simply.

I swallowed hard. "And they've kidnapped my son so they can make him into some kind of... magical overlord? Because in fourteen years, Jace has never shown the slightest hint of magical abilities!"

My stomach turned over as I pictured Jace in the hands of the kind of people who would crucify someone with giant thorns in the public square as a form of punishment.

"He's never showed magical abilities... that you know of," Albigard retorted.

I stared at him. "You're Unseelie, right? So tell me—are you in favor of this? Are you part of the conspiracy? Do you know where the kids are being held?"

The Fae looked pained. "Yes, no, no, and no."

I took a moment to match the answers to the questions, my heart sinking. Not that I truly doubted him. Fae couldn't lie, or so I was told—they could only misdirect. Besides, his people had not only tried to turn him into plant food for a rosebush with an attitude problem; they'd also put some kind of a warding spell on him in an attempt to prevent him from talking about their plan to take over Earth.

Zorah leaned forward in her chair, fingers gripping the armrests. "How the hell did the three of you even manage to get out of Dhuinne alive after all of this?" Her eyes narrowed, landing on me heavily. "The place drives humans insane, Vonnie. You should be a mental vegetable after spending that much time there."

I felt color rising to my cheeks as I struggled valiantly not to think about the hours I'd spent curled naked in Leonides' arms in the darkness, sheltering beneath the protection of his vampire aura to keep Dhuinne's rampaging magic at bay as I slept.

"Human magic offers some protection against the Fae realm's influence," Albigard said.

"And as far as how we got out, that's a bit of a sore point," Leonides muttered.

Zorah's gaze searched first his face, and then mine, before her focus narrowed to my right ear. Instinctively, I lifted a hand, realizing with a jolt that I hadn't thought to remove the emerald earring dangling from my earlobe. The *Fae* earring.

Her breath caught, and she groaned. "Oh, Vonnie, tell me you didn't—" she began.

"Accept a faerie gift and end up acting as an industrial Fae battery charger?" I finished for her, a bit sheepishly. "Um… yeah. 'Fraid so."

"Alby," Rans said, sounding infinitely tired. "You're a conniving, manipulative arse. You know that, right?"

Albigard quirked an eyebrow at him. "You'd have preferred me to stay where I was, so you could all remain ignorant of what is to come?"

Rans gave a frustrated huff.

"What's done is done," Leonides said firmly. "I might not be happy about what Albigard did—or what *Vonnie* did—but it's not like we were gonna leave him there, bound in iron and hanging from giant thorns. At least now we've got answers to some of our questions… if not all of them."

"Quite so," Rans said tightly. "Which leads to a *new* question. What do we do next?"

A knock at the door sounded before the answering silence could grow too stifling.

Leonides made a noise of frustration. "Who the hell is that?"

Albigard waved a listless hand. "It's Nigellus' servant. You know—the wrinkly one. The stench of combined human and demon magic is unmistakable."

I stared at him. "Tact *really* isn't your thing, is it?" I asked mildly.

Leonides checked the security feed before striding to the front door and opening it. I heard him invite Edward inside, and a moment later the elderly demon-bound butler appeared in the living room's archway.

"Oh, good," he said in relief, his eyes running over the room's occupants. "You're all safe."

Leonides scoffed. "I'm not sure *safe* is the first adjective that comes to mind. Anyway, have a seat, Edward. I assume Nigellus dropped you here?"

"Something like that," Edward replied vaguely.

Just as Zorah had done earlier, Edward frowned at me for a few moments before honing in on the Fae earring with unerring accuracy.

"Oh, my dear—you *didn't*," he exclaimed. "After everything I warned you about…"

Clearly, I wasn't going to be living down the *'accepting a Fae gift'* thing anytime soon.

"It was for a good cause," I said, rubbing the heel of my hand against my eye socket in a weary gesture. "Probably."

Edward sighed, his attention moving to Albigard. "I see. Hello, Flight Commander. Circumstances aside, I'm gratified to see you here."

Albigard leaned back in his chair, looking as drained as I felt. "I doubt that particular military title has relevance anymore, demon-slave. Nor can I say with any real degree of truthfulness that it's good to be here."

"Were you able to give our friends the answers they needed?" Edward asked.

I wondered, not for the first time, exactly how much Nigellus actually knew about the Fae plans... and how much of that knowledge he'd passed on to Edward.

"I have given them all the answers I possess... such as they are," Albigard told him. "As for the rest, we were just preparing to discuss the matter when you arrived. I assume the timing is not a co-incidence."

"You give me too much credit, sir," Edward said. "When Ransley and Miss Bright left Atlantic City in the middle of the night without warning, it seemed apparent that there had been some news. This seemed the most likely place to find every-one."

I cringed a bit at the reminder of how I'd kept Zorah and Rans in the dark about our plans to go to Dhuinne—leaving Len with just enough infor-mation to know that we were going into danger, without knowing the details of where or why.

"Yes, and about that," Leonides said. "This is one of the first places anyone will think to come looking for you, Albigard. You'll need to get away from here and hide out someplace less obvious."

Albigard and Rans exchanged a look.

"Chicago?" Rans asked, and the Fae nodded in reply.

"Indeed. I still have access to warded property there. I was, after all, in charge of the Chicago overkeep for a number of years. Those years were not completely wasted when it came to preparing for various contingencies."

Zorah glanced at Rans, her earlier irritation forgotten. "Chicago? Do you think the guys at the *Weekly Oracle* might be able to help figure out where there's been an unusual amount of Fae activity along the ley lines recently?"

"Way ahead of you, love," Rans replied, already rising.

"The *Weekly Oracle*?" I asked, completely lost now.

"It's an underground newspaper run by a group of conspiracy theorists," Zorah explained, rising as well. "They're big on tracking EMF fluctuations, ghost-hunting, that kind of thing. They helped us figure out where the Fae had taken my dad after he disappeared."

"You should all go," Edward said, sounding troubled. "You'd be safer behind wards, and this place is far too obvious a bolt-hole."

But Leonides shook his head. "No... not yet. I'm staying." His tone was hard. "Now that I have a better idea of what's going on, I want another word with Teague. *Several* words, in fact."

TWO

Albigard eyed Leonides doubtfully. "You purposely wish to court the attention of Caspian's replacement? You shouldn't. Whether you realize it or not, you're badly outmatched, vampire."

"Seconded," Edward said, still looking decidedly unhappy. "Up to this point, he's just been toying with you, sir—not to put too fine a point on it. If he learns what you've been doing in Dhuinne, that's likely to change."

"Teague is a hothead," Leonides said. "I've already tangled with him several times, and I know roughly what to expect. He's also our next best source of information. The asshole's neck-deep in this business, and he *knows* where those kids are. It only makes sense to come at the problem from two directions—you go find out what you can in Chicago, and I'll find out what I can on this end."

"I'm staying, too," I blurted. "He's right. We have someone in St. Louis who definitely knows where Jace and the other children are. Teague as much as admitted it to us. We need to pursue that."

"You are both fools, in that case," Albigard said, with a brusquely dismissive gesture implying it was of no real import to him. "Though I suppose that was already obvious after your actions in Dhuinne."

"Perhaps foolhardiness is becoming contagious," Rans offered.

"Look… I'll stay behind as well," Zorah said, not sounding happy about it. "These two might need more backup."

"*Definitely* contagious," Rans muttered.

"Zorah, you don't have to—" I began, only for Zorah to cut me off.

"Shut it, Vonnie," she said. "I love you, babe, but you seriously need to learn to accept help when it's offered."

I paused, closed my mouth, and let that sink in for a moment—knowing how much I was going to need that help.

"Thank you," I told her instead.

Edward's expression wasn't getting any happier. "Do you really think it's wise to openly advertise your involvement in this matter to the Fae, miss? They're not terribly well disposed toward you at the best of times, if you'll recall."

Zorah's lips twisted. "Wise? Probably not. But I get the feeling we're pretty much past the 'stealth' part of the operation, and closer to the 'storming the castle' part. If they haven't figured out already that Rans and I are involved in this mess, they'll realize soon enough. And, if nothing else, Rans is going to be the one directly aiding and abetting an escaped Fae fugitive in Chicago—not me."

"There's danger enough to go around, it's true," Rans agreed in a grudging tone. "So, it's agreed. I'll get Tinkerbell safely to his warded bolt-hole, and while I'm there, I'll set up a meeting with Derek and his mates at the *Weekly Oracle*. You three will stay here and try to pry more information out of Teague, preferably without getting yourselves captured or killed in the process. Edward, I assume you're popping straight back to report all of this to Nigellus, since he can't be bothered to come here and do his own dirty work these days?"

I winced. Clearly, Rans and Zorah's visit to Atlantic City in search of us hadn't done much to quell whatever resentment they held toward the powerful demon of fate.

Edward didn't rise to the bait. "Shortly, sir. I do need a word with Vonnie first, however."

Rans nodded briskly, eyeing Albigard with a critical gaze. "Well, I suppose we'd better be off. Zorah wasn't wrong, mate—you look like complete shit. Are we traveling by portal, or do I need to arrange for some alternate form of transportation?"

Albigard looked like he'd swallowed something sour. "I assume you don't wish me to drain power from a convenient vassal to replenish myself. Otherwise, I'm too weakened to work that kind of magic at the moment."

I suspected I was the 'convenient vassal' in question, so I was relieved when Rans shrugged and said, "No—not unless you want either Guthrie or myself to thrash you into the ground immediately afterward. Let me make a call. I can probably convince Len to let me take the pimpmobile, in exchange for letting him use the Triumph for a week or two."

It was still a slight shock to hear someone refer to Leonides by his decidedly un-vampire-like first name, but I shoved that aside.

Albigard stared at Rans, appalled. "The *what*-mobile? Do I even want to know?" he asked.

"No," Zorah said flatly. "You really don't."

"Nonsense. You'll *love* it," Rans told him. "Carbureted engine, analog everything—it's *just* your speed, Fae."

"Low-key, too," Leonides added, deadpan. "Nothing says 'flying under the radar' like a 1978 Lincoln Continental with chrome wheels, a rusted-out custom paint job, and bullet holes in the quarter-panels."

"It has *character*," I quipped tiredly. "Or so I'm told."

Assuming the old land yacht could actually make it to Chicago without breaking down, it was a more practical choice for the trip than it might have sounded. Fae and advanced technology didn't get along, to put it mildly, and I'd personally seen Teague's presence fry the electronics in modern cars before. Knowing how meticulous Len was about maintaining the Lincoln—bullet holes aside—the pimpmobile probably *could* make the trip. I was just glad I wouldn't be the one paying for all the gasoline it was likely to guzzle in the process.

I was guessing Rans didn't plan on mentioning Albigard's involvement while he was arranging the temporary vehicle trade with Len, given the apparent ugly history between the two. He headed off to make the call, someplace out of Fae cell-phone-frying range.

I took a deep breath and turned my attention to Edward. "So, what did you need to talk to me about?"

The elderly butler straightened in his chair, his clasped hands resting primly on his knees. His white, bushy eyebrows drew together, the lines between them deepening. "Your power signature has changed. I thought at first that accepting the Fae gift might account for it, but there's something else. Your pendant also reads as though it has Fae magic now."

Zorah and Leonides both looked at me. Zorah's eyes narrowed, focusing on the necklace at my throat. "Crap, you're right," she said. "How did I miss that?"

"Probably because the earring reads stronger," Edward offered.

I frowned in surprise, because the pendant felt the same to me as it always had. Then it hit me.

"Oh! It cracked on the way back from Dhuinne," I said. "All the power flowing through it overloaded it, I guess. Albigard fixed it with magic. *Fae* magic. Is that what you're sensing, maybe?"

Edward nodded, his gaze moving to the Fae. "That would certainly explain it. Though you'll pardon me, sir, if I enquire as to whether you made any other changes to the crystal at the same time?"

Albigard had maintained his air of bored detachment during the exchange, but at that, he raised an eyebrow. "As it happens, I did not. It is difficult to avoid leaving fingerprints when fixing broken things, but there should be no change to the item's functionality because of my repairs."

Edward looked at him shrewdly. "Perhaps changes due to some other factor, though?"

The barest twitch of an appreciative smile flitted across Albigard's lips and was gone. It occurred to me that I would need to seriously up my game when it came to dealing with Fae and their careful wording.

"It's true that funneling so much of Dhuinne's magic may have tempered the crystal in new ways," Albigard said casually. "Without returning to the Fae realm, however, it will be difficult to test."

Edward nodded to himself and turned back to me. "I'd like to ward the necklace before I leave, and add a concealment spell. Right now, it's a bit of a beacon, and I fear it may be the sort of beacon that attracts the wrong attention."

I frowned. "You mean something like the misdirection spell you were trying to cast when we were hiding from Teague's SWAT team in the woods? So people wouldn't notice it? That makes sense, I guess. I'm game."

"Very much like that, yes," Edward confirmed. "Though this will place as much emphasis on concealing the pendant's magical signature as its physical appearance."

At that, Albigard looked interested. "Intriguing. I would be interested in the details of craft behind such a spell."

"It will involve blood magic, sir," Edward warned. "I wouldn't wish to offend your sensibilities."

Albigard waved him off. "I've spilled enough of the stuff recently, demon-slave. Let us say that the novelty has begun to wear off."

Both Zorah and Leonides looked mystified by the exchange.

"Do Fae have a problem with blood magic?" Zorah asked.

I remembered Len telling Albigard, '*Get some rest and, I dunno, drink lots of water or something. Or maybe vampire blood, if that shit even works on your kind.*'

Albigard's eyes had narrowed before he shot back, '*I would rather suffer these wounds a thousand times over than drink the blood of a vampire.*'

At the time, I'd taken it as more evidence of Fae prejudice and xenophobia... but now I wondered if it had more to do with the *blood* aspect than the *vampire* aspect.

"Fae have a problem with demon magic," Albigard told Zorah. "And, by extension, with vampire magic, which resides wholly in the blood. By contrast, pure human magic—such as it is—descended originally from Fae magic. This demon-corrupted human uses a mixture of both varieties. It is offensive, admittedly... but nonetheless interesting."

"Know thine enemy?" Leonides suggested tartly.

Albigard scoffed. "The old man is not my enemy. Not currently, at least."

Not for the first time, I wondered if tact was even a concept among the Fae. If it was, I hadn't seen much evidence of it to date.

"I'm fine with it if you are, Edward," I said. "After all, I already gave him a creepy connection to my soul."

"Join the club," Zorah muttered, and I looked at her sharply.

"Very well," Edward said, slapping his thighs briskly and rising on creaky knees. "Perhaps on the patio, in that case. Mr. Leonides, if you and Ms. Bright wouldn't mind staying here — there's nothing particularly secretive about the process, but it does become more complicated, the more magical auras are in the immediate vicinity."

I rose with him, shooting a furtive glance at Leonides, only to look away quickly when I found him watching me in turn. There was another conversation that needed to happen between us, I knew — but I'd be damned if I was having it in public, with witnesses. Albigard dragged himself upright as well, swaying for a moment before his balance steadied.

He still looked... *wrong* in his borrowed button-down shirt and trousers. The fit of the clothing wasn't too bad; he was roughly the same height as Leonides, if a bit more lithe. Even without the pointed ears, though, it somehow seemed like he should be wearing leather and buckskin and flowing linen, not sharply tailored wool and cotton.

We left the room as Zorah rounded on Leonides, probably revving up to try and wring more answers out of him about what had happened in Dhuinne. In this particular instance, I was happy enough to throw him under the bus, at least for the time being. I knew I still owed Zorah more in the way of both explanation and apology. Len, too, when he was eventually ready to hear it.

That didn't mean I was looking forward to either of those conversations.

Right now, I could barely get my brain around the bigger things that were happening. If I stopped long enough for what I'd learned to truly begin to penetrate, I'd be overwhelmed... and I couldn't afford to be overwhelmed right now. So, I was back to putting one foot in front of the other. Keep moving forward; that was the key.

Let Edward protect my pendant as best he could.

Let Rans pull Albigard out of the crosshairs we'd aimed at him.

Help Leonides draw Teague into the open, in hopes that we'd have more luck prying information out of him this time than we'd had last time.

Get Jace back.

There was such a vast gulf separating the last item on that list from the others that I nearly panicked again—the air around me swirling weakly as my depleted magic stirred. I took slow, deep breaths as Albigard led the way through the sliding glass door and onto the rooftop patio with its gas fire pit, swim spa, and huge hot tub. Edward sat me down on one of the lounges and rummaged in his pocket for a knife.

He lifted it up, the point glinting in the last rays of evening sunlight as Albigard looked on with clear interest.

"Now, my dear," Edward asked politely. "I believe you know the drill by now. Which do you prefer... left arm or right?"

THREE

Forty-five minutes and several blood-sigils later, Albigard tilted his head like a cat, his eyes fixed firmly on my boobs.

"Fascinating," he said, almost certainly *not* in reference to my breasts. He tore his eyes away to meet Edward's gaze. "What is the latency surrounding such a spell? Surely it cannot be permanent, given the competing magical classes involved in casting it."

"Not permanent, no," Edward agreed. "A few weeks, perhaps. Less if the sigil is damaged or removed."

I craned down to confirm my earlier impression that the necklace was still hanging beneath the hollow of my throat like it always did—just a little more blood-smeared than usual. "Erm… no offense, guys, but am I missing something? I can feel the warding… I think. But it doesn't look very *concealed* from where I'm standing."

Edward chuckled. "That's because you're inside the spell." He gestured toward the patio door. "Look at your reflection in the glass."

I crossed to the door and did as he'd told me—only to gasp faintly in surprise. In the reflection, my hand flew up to brush across nothing. In reality, I felt the solid warmth of the magic-infused garnet. Remembering what Edward had said about the tiny sigil drawn in our combined blood, I pulled my fingers away, not wanting to damage it accidentally.

The image in the glass showed only bare skin and a dark cotton t-shirt where the weight of the pendant and gold chain hung. It was hard to look at the area for long—my eyes wanted to skitter away and focus on something else. *Anything* else.

"Wow," I said brilliantly. "Okay, that's pretty impressive. So, um, how careful do I have to be about anything touching it, so I don't damage the sigil?"

"I put as much magical protection over it as I could," Edward replied. "Casual touch won't harm it. Sacred waters probably wouldn't do it much good, and I'd avoid getting salt on it."

"Shouldn't be a problem," I promised. "At least, not unless things get even crazier than they are now." I paused. "Which, y'know, is possible, I guess."

"Occupational hazard," Edward offered sympathetically. He fussed with his cuffs, straightening them, and checked his watch. "Well, I suppose I must be getting on. I daresay it's useless to harp on the subject, but do *please* be careful if you truly insist on staying here. It really isn't safe."

I turned away from the misleading reflection in the patio door, and stepped forward to give him a brief hug. "It's not safe anywhere, Edward. Not for us... not now. That much has become obvious over the past few weeks. Besides, I'll have Leonides and Zorah looking out for me."

Edward patted my back before extricating himself. "Indeed. Be careful nonetheless, my dear." He dipped his head in Albigard's direction. "Farewell, sir. I look forward to discussing magic with you in more depth at some future date."

"I would find such a discussion illuminating, I think," Albigard replied thoughtfully.

With a last formal little half-bow, Edward took his leave and disappeared into the apartment. Rather than follow him inside, I moved to the lounge where I'd been sitting earlier and addressed a question to Albigard — one that had been nagging at me.

"What did you mean earlier about human magic being descended from Fae magic?"

He regarded me with tired green eyes. "A pet theory, nothing more. One which would cause serious offense in many places on Dhuinne."

"Oh? Go on. What's this offensive theory, then?" I pressed.

He leaned back, his gaze assessing. "Some of Dhuinne's greatest thinkers over the centuries have postulated that Fae occasionally interbred with early humans, producing hybrid offspring with a weaker, bastardized form of magic. The very idea of such a thing is nauseating, of course."

I raised an eyebrow at him. "Of course."

After mulling the idea over for a few minutes, however, I decided it was all too easy to picture some credulous bronze age Celtic maiden succumbing to the lure of the unnaturally beautiful and magnetic Unseelie. Not that I was about to feed Albigard's ego by saying so aloud.

"Okay, next question," I said instead. "I've got an invisible magical pendant now. What the hell am I supposed to do with it? Teague already knows about the necklace. He knows it's what allows me to shake off his influence, and he's been able to influence me when I wasn't wearing it in the past."

Albigard appeared to give it a few moments' thought. "Assuming he's unable to penetrate the concealment spell and the wards, he will believe you to be vulnerable when he sees you without it. I suppose the question is whether you would rather have him think you weak, or have him believe you are growing in strength to the extent that you no longer require a focus for your power."

I considered that. "I think, given the choice, I want him off balance."

The Fae nodded. "You will be a target either way—albeit a target of a different sort, should he believe you to be unnaturally powerful for a human."

"I *am* unnaturally powerful for a human," I said. "Or so I've been told."

Albigard tilted his chin, acknowledging the point. "Perhaps, adept. Presently, though, you are drained... as I am."

"And whose fault is that?" I asked, not trying to hide the irony lacing my tone.

He gave a slow blink. "An interesting philosophical question. *You* were the one who accepted my gift."

"You were the one who offered it in the first place," I shot back. "Maybe I should throw it back in your face right now."

A lazy smirk tugged at one corner of his lips. "That is not how such arrangements work, as I suspect you're already aware. Besides, so far you seem to be a much more convenient and useful acquisition than the demonkin has been."

I scowled at him. "Demon... kin? Wait, you mean *Zorah*? Did you seriously pull this trick on her, too?"

"Oh, yes—some time ago," he said immediately. "And I've been regretting it ever since."

The sound of the glass door sliding open and closed drew my attention away from him before I could come up with a suitable reply to that.

"My ears are burning," Zorah said as she joined us. "You know I can sense gossip at a hundred paces, right?"

But Albigard had already retreated into his usual haughty aloofness. "Truly, your crossbreed talents know no bounds."

"Not true," she retorted. "I've got plenty of bounds. I still can't make a decent quiche, for one thing. Not that there's much point in attempting it, these days." Her attention turned to me. "The good news is, Guthrie apparently *can* make a decent quiche. You should go take advantage of it while it's still warm."

My stomach rumbled, helpfully reminding me that it was getting late and I was hungry.

"Right. Food. Food is good." I glanced between them. "Will you two be all right out here? You're not going to have some kind of vampire-Fae smackdown as soon as I leave?"

Zorah's eyebrows went up. "What—me and Tinkerbell? Nah, don't be ridiculous. We're like *that*." She lifted a hand, her index and middle fingers crossed tightly to demonstrate. "It's him and Rans that are always trying to skewer each other with pointy objects. They love each other really, though."

Albigard shot her a deeply offended look, like a cat that had just been forced into a bathtub and lathered with shampoo.

Zorah pinned my gaze and held it. "You and me, though? That's a different matter. We've got some issues to hash out, and we're going to talk. *Soon*."

I bit my lip and nodded. "Yeah. Soon." And then I fled inside like the coward I was, following the savory smell of egg, cheese, and spinach to the kitchen.

Leonides was waiting for me.

"Rans left to pick up Len's car," he said. "He should be back soon." His eyes dipped to my throat. "Huh. That's pretty uncanny. You're really still wearing the garnet?"

I lifted it by the chain, letting it dangle invisibly between two fingers. "Yup. Edward knows his stuff, all right."

Leonides shook his head and transferred a couple of wedges of quiche to a plate, sliding it toward me. "It's weird, isn't it? I mean, don't get me wrong. I've seen some shit—especially over the last few months. But the David Copperfield routine still gets to me, you know? It's like... it's one thing when a demon or a Fae does something impossible before breakfast. But when the doddering old butler starts throwing balls of light around and making things invisible… *that's* disconcerting."

A snort of tired laughter jerked free from my lips, even though there wasn't a single damned thing in my life that was funny right now.

"Yeah," I agreed. "Honestly? I think he even impressed Albigard with his magic."

I sat down and dug into the quiche. It was good. The silence stretched, and I grew ever more acutely aware that I was alone with Leonides for the first time since I'd woken up wrapped in his arms in a Fae cottage, smelling of sex and desperation and the morning after.

I put the fork down and cleared my throat.

"So. Are we going to talk about…? Well, you know."

He went still. "Which aspect?"

I stared at him, trying to figure out if he was serious or not. "Uh. Which aspect do you *think*?"

There was an uncomfortable pause.

"I hadn't really planned on it, no," he said eventually, still holding himself unmoving. "Just let it be what it is, Vonnie. Sex doesn't have to be complicated. And it doesn't have to have a deeper meaning."

That wasn't sex, though, I wanted to say. *That was… what? A pity orgasm? And a decidedly one-sided pity orgasm, at that.*

But then footsteps were approaching from the hall, and it was too late. My ears heated as I wondered how much of the exchange Zorah's vampire hearing had picked up. Leonides looked away, busying himself in serving up a second plate of food, which he shoved toward Albigard when the Fae entered.

Thankfully for my already tattered self-esteem, Zorah didn't say anything about the interrupted conversation. I stuffed my face with food to cover my discomfort, while Albigard picked at his plate as though Earth cuisine wasn't good enough for his refined Fae palate.

Rans arrived soon after we finished the awkward meal, lifting a key ring with a set of fuzzy dice hanging from it and letting it dangle in Albigard's line of sight like a challenge.

He smiled, showing fang. It wasn't a friendly expression. "Right, Tinkerbell. When's the last time you went on an epic American Midwest road trip?"

FOUR

Before he left, Rans disappeared into one of the bedrooms with Zorah for fifteen minutes. When she reappeared with him as he and Albigard were preparing to go, it was with a definite air of dishevelment hastily put to rights.

She'd missed two buttons on her corset-top.

I caught myself staring and looked away, trying not to wonder what it must be like to be the kind of person who jumped their lover's bones for a quickie in someone else's apartment before the lover in question headed off to a different city.

It was true I could no longer claim *complete* ignorance about the appeal of sex. Orgasms were really nice. If I weren't desperately trying to get my son back while simultaneously preventing evil Fae from taking over the world, I'd probably enjoy having them on at least a somewhat regular basis. But that kind of spontaneous, up-against-the-wall passion still seemed incomprehensible to me.

"If you three insist on sitting here in St. Louis with targets painted on your backs," Rans was saying, "then I would at least suggest taking action to minimize any potential collateral damage."

"Already on it," Leonides replied. "Though I've gotta say, I'm surprised you're not raising more of a fuss about Zorah staying behind."

Rans shrugged a careless shoulder, his blue eyes landing on her warmly for a moment before returning to Leonides. "We might be soul-bound, but that doesn't make her my possession, mate. She makes her own decisions. And as long as Nigellus is around, it's not as though her life is in any real danger, now is it?"

My brow furrowed in confusion, but the others seemed to understand what he was talking about. Leonides huffed out a breath. "I guess that's one way of looking at it. All right—get going, you two assholes. Try not to wreck Len's car."

"Or stab each other," Zorah added cheerfully. "*No stabbing*. Just think of this as uninterrupted male bonding time!"

Rans eyed Albigard with a jaundiced expression, which the Fae returned in kind. The vampire cleared his throat. "Yes. Quite."

Albigard's lip curled in distaste. "Perhaps the iron collar and the thorn-prison were not so unappealing after all."

"I can book a flight to Ireland for us and drop you back in County Meath if you'd prefer, Tinkerbell," Rans said pointedly.

The Fae's nostrils flared in irritation.

After they left and Leonides closed the door behind them, Zorah sighed.

"They love each other, really," she repeated gamely.

"Uh-huh," I said in a skeptical tone, wondering how much likelihood there was that the two would arrive in Chicago without any physical violence along the way. Shaking it off, I turned to her.

"So... what was that part about soul-bonds and Nigellus, exactly?"

Her expression turned sour. "Oh. That. Short version—Rans sold his soul to Nigellus in the eighteenth century, but he made Nigellus remove the memory of doing it as part of the deal. Later, he trapped me in a life-bond as a ploy to get me safely out of Dhuinne. That's kind of like what demons do to claim souls, but since neither of us are immortal, the practical upshot is that if one of us dies, we both do."

"*What*?" I blurted, appalled.

She waved me off. "Yeah, yeah, I know—it's all very Romeo and Juliet. But, in our case, the first part kind of cancels out the second. Nigellus needs an ongoing source of vampire blood, and we're it. Plus, he likes Rans. So, he's not about to let Rans die, and that means he's not going to let me die, by extension. I wish I could say we haven't already had cause to put that theory to the test, but..."

"They have," Leonides finished. His expression was grim. "I'll admit, I struggle to find anything positive to say about demons or demon-bonds, but if they have any kind of an upside, that would be it."

Zorah nodded. "And vampires are already tough to start with. Suffice to say, it's not *me* you two should be worrying about."

I remembered ancient, frail Edward—wounded in the shoulder with a high-powered rifle round that would later heal miraculously. Remembered him reassuring me that the men hunting us couldn't do anything to him 'that would stick.'

Turning to Leonides, I tried to fit this new revelation into the growing puzzle picture of the supernatural world.

"You're demon-bound, too," I said slowly. "That's why you weren't aging, even before you were turned."

He made a disgruntled noise. "True, but Myrial's not really in a position to put me back together if I get broken. Mind you, I'm also not sure whether he's in a position to slurp my life force up through a straw if I manage to get myself killed, either... but it's not really something I'm in a hurry to test."

I nodded, aware that the demon to whom Leonides was bound didn't seem to possess the same level of beneficence as Nigellus when it came to the souls he owned. "Since we're playing Twenty Paranormal Questions, here's another one for you. Sometimes you call Myrial 'he,' and sometimes 'she.' What's up with that?" I asked.

It was Zorah who answered. "Myrial is a succubus... or an incubus, as circumstances dictate. In fact, in a sense Myrial is also my dear old grandpappy—the one who stole Guthrie's DNA and used it to get my grandmother pregnant with my mother. Incubi and succubi can change sex at will."

I stared at her, blinking. "Oh. And... can you...?"

She grinned, sharp and lethal. "Not so much. I'm just a lowly second-generation hybrid. When I want boy parts, I have to use a strap-on."

"Too much information, Zorah," Leonides said in an absolutely flat tone.

She shrugged, unrepentant. "*Hey*. She asked."

I judged it probably not worth the effort to point out that I'd asked about her magical abilities, not her adventurous sex life. Besides, it was already taking too much concentration to keep track of everything else I'd learned today.

"Okay. So, Edward and Rans are both bound to Nigellus, and you kind of are by extension, Zorah, because you're bound to Rans. Leonides is bound to this demon Myrial, who's currently hanging out in a bunch of bloody pieces, stashed in multiple bags of salt and scattered around the world. Zorah also accepted a gift from Albigard, and so did I," I recited. "Am I missing anyone? Len's not wrapped up with Albigard somehow, is he?"

Zorah let out a startled bark of laughter. "Len? Uh, *no*. Len punched Albigard in the jaw after Albigard tried to influence him once. That's pretty much the extent of their relationship."

"I expect he only did it because he was hopped up on cocaine at the time," Leonides muttered. "Apparently strong stimulants have a protective effect against Fae manipulation, at least for some people."

I supposed that went some way toward explaining the obvious friction between the pair.

"Right. You know, this all seems very…" I began, only to trail off, searching for the right word.

"Incestuous?" Leonides offered.

"Complicated," I settled on. With a deep breath, I refocused. "So, what next? Do we have any sort of a plan here, beyond sitting around and hoping our presence pisses Teague off enough to draw him out? Because I need to make some calls, and it's just occurred to me that my cell phone is sitting in an abandoned rental car in a parking lot in rural Ireland."

At least my keys had still been in my pocket when Albigard unceremoniously portaled us across the Atlantic. That was something, I supposed.

"I should arrange some things with Gina," Leonides said. "But beyond that, yes, I expect it will be a waiting game. Though probably not a very long one, after what happened in Dhuinne with Albigard."

I nodded. "Okay. In that case, I want to go back to my apartment for a bit. I should follow up with some of Richard's friends. As much as I frequently fantasize about him dying in a dumpster fire, it's making me nervous not knowing where he is."

It said something about the past few weeks that the father of my child manifesting terrifying magical abilities, killing a bunch of armed men, then running off and disappearing to who-knew-where, was actually kind of low on my list of things to worry about. Still, I'd feel better knowing Richard was licking his wounds on a buddy's couch, rather than undergoing torture at the hands of the Fae, or, y'know, lying dead in a random ditch somewhere.

"I'll go to your apartment with you," Zorah said. "Guthrie, get the woman a new burner phone first, will you?"

Leonides grunted, and pushed away from the wall he'd been propping up.

"Do you seriously keep a drawer full of burner phones in your office?" I couldn't help asking.

"Doesn't everyone?" he replied as he headed deeper in the penthouse, and I couldn't tell if he was joking or not.

Zorah's voice turned wry. "Yeah... he once set Rans and me up with new forged identities in, like, ten minutes flat, credit cards included. I think he keeps all that shit in a file cabinet somewhere. Don't let him fool you — my gramps is a stone cold gangster when he's not listening to jazz or managing stocks and bonds for people."

I scrubbed at my face. "Yeah, I figured that part out not long after he made a guy who was stalking one of his employees disappear. Permanently."

Zorah was silent for a beat. "I'm guessing the guy in question deserved it?"

I pondered that for a moment. "He wanted to hurt Kat — she's one of the bartenders. He stabbed Len when Len got between them to protect her. Honestly, I was afraid Len was going to die." I swallowed hard. "That was the night I learned Leonides was a vampire. Well... it was the night the information stuck with me, anyway."

"It's a different world, in so many ways," Zorah offered. "I think a lot of it's because of the lifespan. Having a ridiculously long lifespan messes with how you see life and death."

Leonides returned with a phone that looked brand new, not to mention far more expensive than anything I would have gotten for myself.

"Here you go. Hopefully your contacts are backed up in the cloud," he said. "If not, I've got someone in Ireland taking care of the abandoned rental car. They'll ship all our personal items back here, though it will take some time since it's international."

For the hundredth time, I wondered what it must be like to be *that* rich.

"Okay," I said. "I think most of my contacts are on my Google account. If not, there's an address book in the apartment with the important ones written down."

"Old school. I like it," he said approvingly. "Go on, you two. Don't take too long, though. I'm not thrilled with the idea of us being split up whenever the next round of Fae shit decides to hit the turboprop."

"We won't," Zorah replied, before I could say anything. "Come on, babe. Is your car here?"

So much had happened since we'd left for Atlantic City that I had to stop and think for a moment. "Um… yeah. It's in the parking garage. Hopefully with enough charge left on the battery to start."

"I had a guy come here and replace your battery and alternator while we were out of town," Leonides said, as though that was the kind of thing people just *did*. "Easier than having to give you a jump every time you need to go anywhere."

I opened my mouth to protest, thought for a moment, and closed it. "Um... thanks?" I said instead.

Zorah patted my shoulder. "There ya go. You're learning, hon."

FIVE

At some point in the past few weeks, I'd started worrying every time I was away from my apartment that I would come back to find the door broken down and all my stuff gone. Happily, that wasn't the case when Zorah and I arrived at the run-down building.

"I just need to get another bag packed and call a few of Richard's friends to see if they've heard anything from him," I said, after a quick check to make sure everything inside was as I'd left it.

Zorah threw herself onto the squishy couch and put her feet up on the coffee table. "Cool," she said. "I'll just hang out here and contemplate how best to yell at you some more about the Dhuinne stunt."

I sighed. "You do that."

My selection of clean clothing and toiletries was getting a bit sparse after so much time spent living out of a bag recently. And speaking of my overnight bag, it was also in Ireland. *Wonderful.* I entered Jace's room and grabbed his spare school backpack, my heart contracting in a painful spasm as I did.

It terrified me that as the days rolled on, I found myself sometimes going hours at a time without thinking about my child. Without thinking about him being *gone*. Would that get worse over time, like mourning a death, all the while gradually getting back to your life whether you wanted to or not?

Because I didn't think I could take that. I didn't *want* to mourn Jace. I wanted to *find* him.

My knees went weak, and I sank down on the edge of his bed. The blankets didn't smell like him anymore. His scent had dissipated into the atmosphere... *gone*. I took a breath, but it caught and made an ugly noise in my throat.

And... now I was crying. Again.

Fuck.

I let the backpack drop and covered my face with one hand. The scuff of a boot against carpet let me know Zorah had come into the room. She sighed and came to a stop in front of me. When I didn't look up, she settled on the floor with her back to me, her shoulder leaning casually against my left leg.

"Okay," she said. "I won't yell at you after all. But we're still talking about this."

I sniffled and nodded, dragging myself under some semblance of control.

"Nigellus specifically told Leonides not to let you know we were visiting him," I tried to explain, a bit hoarsely. "But I thought if Len knew, and something happened..."

"He'd tell us, and we'd shout at him instead of shouting at you," she finished. "Yeah, I already figured out that part, thanks."

"I thought it was just because you two were pissed at Nigellus and he didn't want to deal with the drama," I continued. "That's what Leonides made it sound like. But Nigellus already knew we'd be going to Dhuinne. And I get the impression it would be dangerous for either of you to get near the place. Like… *more* dangerous, I mean. That's why he didn't want you involved, I'm guessing?"

Zorah was quiet for a moment before answering.

"The Fae took my dad and spirited him away to Dhuinne. They did it to get to *me*, because I'm a hybrid who isn't supposed to exist. As far as they're concerned, I'm an abomination. At first, I thought I could be a hero… trade myself for Dad; get them to let him go. It was a trap, of course. But I talked Albigard into taking me to Dhuinne behind Rans' back. That's what splintered their friendship, by the way. *Me*. Or at least, my issues."

I frowned, caught up in the story. "What happened to you?"

"The Fae took me into custody and tortured me, nearly to death… using magic to try and figure out how I'd come to be conceived. My mother was a cambion—a half-demon—and cambions are supposed to be sterile. They didn't find anything useful. They just hurt me. And when they finally gave up trying, I would have been executed by beheading on the order of the Court… if Rans hadn't showed up like some dark, avenging angel and gotten me out by claiming me in a life-bond."

"Oh," I said blankly.

"I won't say all Fae are inherently evil," she continued. "Albigard isn't. The cat-*sidhe* isn't. But they're ruthless, and they mostly consider human beings to be cattle, rather than people. You two went there without telling anyone. Or, rather, you went without telling *us*. I imagine Guthrie had Gina or someone else in the loop, just in case."

"I didn't want to put you in more danger," I said weakly, aware of how shitty it would be to find out that your friends were cluelessly traipsing into a place where you'd once been tortured and almost killed. "Len said you went to Atlantic City. Did Nigellus tell you where we were?"

"No, he didn't." Zorah's voice was grim. "Though it was pretty obvious you must either be in Dhuinne or Hell. We were about to start working on Edward, when Guthrie called to say you were back here in St. Louis with Albigard."

"I won't apologize," I said. "I just want to get Jace back without anyone else I care about getting hurt."

Zorah reached around awkwardly to pat my thigh. "I know, babe. Believe me, I *know*. But you've gotta believe me when I say this isn't the way to do it." She craned up to meet my gaze. "Please tell me you get that part now?"

I closed my eyes, still feeling completely overwhelmed by the situation we were facing. "How the hell are we supposed to fix this mess?" I whispered, even though it wasn't an answer.

"I dunno yet," she said. "Not exactly, anyway. But I'm guessing the answer includes the word 'together.' So no more sneaking off, all right?"

Could I promise her that, and mean it? Perhaps more to the point, would Zorah even let me out of this apartment if I didn't?

"Okay," I replied.

She smiled, quick and bright as her namesake. "Good girl. Now, let's get you packed, and you can call the waste-of-space ex's buddies so we can get back to Guthrie's place. That's where the action will end up being, I suspect."

I took a deep breath and nodded, accepting her cool hand as she rose and pulled me to my feet. I led the way back to my bedroom, only to nearly trip over myself when she added, "Oh, and by the way—two thumbs up on finally getting *you-know-who* into bed. You *go*, girl."

Heat rushed to my cheeks, sharp and tingling. "What? How…?"

Smooth, Vonnie, I thought. *Way to play it off. Real subtle.*

Zorah waggled her eyebrows. "Succubus, remember? Let's just say it's in the blood."

I could've tried to explain what had happened… to tell her it wasn't like that, and there probably wouldn't be a repeat. Like, *ever*. But that prospect was ever so slightly more mortifying than keeping my mouth shut and letting her make assumptions. So, instead, I clenched my jaw, marched into my room, and started throwing clothes in the backpack. I thought I heard a faint huff of amusement behind me, and pointedly ignored it.

Once everything was packed, I took Albigard's earring out of my ear and laid it on the bedside table. Doing so wouldn't affect the deal I'd made with him, but I wasn't sure I wanted the constant reminder while wearing it. I also didn't know what Teague might make of it when he inevitably showed up.

Setting up the new burner phone and logging into my cloud account took some time. As soon as the contacts were synced, I started placing calls. No one had seen Richard since a few days ago, when he'd stopped by Clint's place to borrow fifty bucks. I supposed that was better than nothing. At least as of then, he'd been okay, for the typical 'Richard' definition of okay.

"Well," I said, pocketing the phone, "I guess if he's in danger, he can just conjure a terrifying spectral wolf again. Could be worse."

Zorah shook her head. "That whole thing is really crazy, you know? What are the odds of you two getting together like that—both of you with magic, but not knowing it?"

I shrugged. "Not much different than any other coincidence, I guess. If Rans hadn't given both of us vampire blood, who knows? We might never have manifested any powers at all."

My fingertips brushed the invisible crystal hanging at my throat, and I focused inward, feeling its reassuring metaphysical hum.

"S'pose so," Zorah agreed after a moment's thought. "Okay. If you're done, let's get back to the penthouse and see what's happening there."

What was happening was... nothing. Like, *aggressively* nothing. The building's parking garage was empty except for Leonides' little BMW convertible, Zorah's motorcycle, and a handful of vaguely familiar looking cars that I guessed belonged to tenants in the other apartments.

"Huh," Zorah said. "Guess he must've listened to Rans about minimizing potential collateral damage."

The club downstairs was eerily quiet, devoid of either staff or patrons. The security cameras followed us with disconcerting red-lit eyes, only the hum of the HVAC system breaking the silence on the floor. Most of the lights were off.

Upstairs, Leonides greeted us as though nothing were amiss, gesturing at us to come in, and offering to take my backpack to the guest room for me. I waved him off and took it myself, dropping it unceremoniously onto the bed before returning to join the others.

"Did Gina suddenly decide to get out of the nightclub business?" I asked.

"The building's undergoing emergency renovation," he replied, absolutely deadpan. "Apparently there was some structural fire damage that didn't get flagged in the initial inspection."

I leveled a flat stare at him, wondering if the embarrassment had *finally* been burned out of me due to repeated exposure... or if I was just really, really tired right now.

"Convenient," I said. "I sure hope the insurance covers it."

"So everyone's gone?" Zorah asked. "There are still a few cars in the parking garage."

"No, not everyone," Leonides replied. "The club's closed. The other tenants have been advised that things might be unpleasant for a few days with the contractors coming in to do work, and that they'd be more comfortable at a hotel. Difficult to actually force them to leave if they don't want to, though."

"What's Teague likely to do next, do you think?" I asked them both. In my head, I'd pictured another confrontation similar to our previous ones, but Leonides seemed to be bracing for something more serious than that.

Up to this point, he's just been toying with you, sir — not to put too fine a point on it, Edward had warned him. *If he learns what you've been doing in Dhuinne, that's likely to change.*

Unease had been living in my stomach for so long that it had become a normal part of my daily existence. Worrying about Teague was just another facet of it, even now. If it meant getting any sort of fresh clue about Jace, I decided I'd face whatever he brought down on us, with Leonides and Zorah at my side.

"Not sure," Leonides said. "If I had to guess, he'll try to interrogate us to find out where Albigard went. Or possibly just try to capture us. Fortunately, Zorah and I have already had a fair amount of practice at not being captured by Fae."

"And to think, I've only been killed once during the attempt," Zorah said grimly. "So our track record is, uh... pretty good, I guess?"

"Well, if you hadn't tried to drain all four of them at once..." Leonides began, like it was an old argument.

"Yeah, yeah—everyone's a critic," Zorah groused. "But for what it's worth, sucking Fae animus can't kill me anymore; it can only give me indigestion. So there's that."

I tried to take this new information on board. "Okay. So if things really start to go south, we'll plan on Leonides shooting iron bullets at Teague. Meanwhile, I'll throw magic at him—which he won't be expecting, because it looks like I'm not wearing my pendant—and you'll... drink his blood?"

Zorah gave a short laugh. "No, babe. I don't fight with my fangs. I fight succubus style, by drawing out people's life force—their animus—through their chakra points. Though, I just want to say up front that Fae animus tastes like moldy diarrhea."

"Right..." I said, wondering exactly when I'd fallen into an X-Men movie.

"The point is, if we can turn the tables on him, *we'll* be the ones doing the interrogating," Leonides said, with a kind of sharpness in his expression that sent a little shiver down my spine. It worried me that my body couldn't seem to decide if it was a good shiver or a bad shiver.

"So, now we wait," Zorah said.

"Yes," Leonides agreed. "Now we wait."

If you'd asked me two months ago whether I'd ever find myself watching *Lucifer* on Netflix in a swanky penthouse, with a smirking vampire-succubus hybrid sprawled against my shoulder, I would have looked at you like you were crazy.

As it was, I was pretty sure Zorah had chosen the show as some kind of subtle dig at me—hot nightclub owner, overworked single mom, supernatural shenanigans. Leonides had disappeared almost immediately into his office to 'take care of some things.' and I didn't blame him one bit.

We were midway into the third episode when Zorah craned around to look at me.

"You should really go talk to him," she said.

And… um, yeah. Hard *no* on that.

"He's busy," I said. "And talking isn't really our thing, in case that wasn't already obvious."

She gave me an unimpressed look. "Huh. Sounds like you need more practice, in that case."

I shifted away a few inches on the couch. "Zorah. Sweetheart. I know you're just trying to help, but this thing you think is happening? It's not happening. There were… some weird circumstances in Dhuinne, and my judgment was maybe… not the best. He's a great guy. A bit emotionally constipated, I mean… but still."

She snorted softly.

I plowed on gamely. "Trust me when I say, it meant nothing to him. And trust me when I say, I've got enough on my plate at the moment without adding *that* kind of thing into the mix. So while I appreciate what you're trying to do—"

I broke off, my pendant tingling against my chest. An instant later, Zorah sat bolt upright, her face going as intent as a hunting wolf's.

"Shit," she said. "We've got Fae somewhere in the building."

SIX

"Guthrie!" Zorah called, as I scrambled off the couch, pendant in hand. It was still glowing warm against my fingers, but not with the same urgent pulse of heat I'd felt on previous occasions when Teague was nearby and focusing his magic on me.

Leonides strode in from the hallway, stowing a semiautomatic pistol in a shoulder holster as he approached. "Where are they? Can either of you tell?"

"Somewhere below us," Zorah said. "Though, seeing as we're in the penthouse, I realize that's not super-helpful."

"Not too close to us, I don't think," I added, fairly confident of that fact.

His eyes flicked to Zorah. "You armed?"

She drew a dagger made of dark metal from a sheath hidden at her back—iron. I hadn't even noticed she was wearing it.

"Vonnie?" he asked. "How's your magic?"

I lifted my chin. "It's coming back now that Albigard's gone and I've had a few hours to rest. I can probably throw someone against a wall if I have to."

Of course, whether that extended to throwing a *Fae* against the wall was an entirely different question, but I was banking on my apparent lack of a magical focus giving me the element of surprise if it came down to a fight. With luck, though, our Fae gadfly was just here to bitch at us and threaten us some more.

"Right. Let's go downstairs and see what the asshole has to say," I said, pretending cockiness I didn't truly feel.

"Stairs," Zorah said. "It'll be easier for me to track him that way."

"He's probably in the club," Leonides offered. "That's been the pattern so far, at least."

The emergency stairwell was just about the only place in the building that hadn't recently been renovated within an inch of its life. It was just like every other emergency stairwell in every other old, multi-story building in St. Louis—an architect's ode to concrete and uninspiring paint choices. That being said, the door hinges were at least oiled, and the handle turned smoothly—the latch releasing with a solid *click* as we entered.

Zorah paused at each landing, only to shake her head and say, "Nope. Lower."

All I could say with certainty was that whatever magic was present, it wasn't right on top of us. The necklace continued to hum a low warning, but nothing more. I was huffing and puffing by the time we reached the ground floor and exited into the club. The echoing space was silent and still, just as it had been earlier. Deserted.

"No," Zorah said. "This isn't right, it's still below us." She looked around in confusion. "Or at least, it *was*. I'm barely getting anything now. You, Von?"

I tried to interpret the ambiguous buzz of power. "Um... I can't really tell. It's definitely no stronger than it was when we were in the penthouse, and it seems like it should be, now that we're closer. I can still sense *something*, though."

Leonides drew his handgun and checked it. "Okay. Let's keep going, in that case."

"What's below us?" Zorah asked. "There's just the parking garage, right?"

"The parking garage is on top of the mechanical floor," he said. "Boiler, HVAC, that kind of thing."

Zorah's lip curled into an unhappy expression. "So, in other words, the setting for the climactic scene in one out of every four horror movies ever made since the beginning of time? Terrific."

Leonides only grunted in reply, already heading back to the stairwell. Zorah and I followed. The parking garage was just as quiet and undisturbed as the club had been. I took a deep breath and let it out, feeling my trepidation grow as we jogged down the final flight of stairs. Whatever we'd sensed, it must be here, on the lowest level.

"Stay here," Zorah said, when we reached the landing. "I'll do a sweep, see if any Fae are still in there."

With that, her body dissipated into a swirl of mist that flowed through the tiny gaps around the door. I waited next to Leonides, tense and silent, trying to make sense of the nebulous awareness of magic that still seemed to be all around me — albeit at a barely detectable level. Leonides still had his gun drawn, though it was pointed at the ground and his finger wasn't on the trigger. He appeared to be listening intently, though all I could hear beyond the closed door was the undifferentiated clamor of industrial machinery.

I jumped when the door opened, but it only revealed Zorah.

"No Fae here," she said. "But you two need to come and see this."

Leonides stowed the gun and headed out, following Zorah's lead as she wove her way through the maze of pipes and ductwork. I felt jumpy as hell as I tagged along behind them, still clutching the garnet hanging invisibly at my neck as though the crystal was some kind of a lifeline.

"What is it?" Leonides asked. "What did you see?"

"I have absolutely no freaking clue what it is," Zorah replied. "Easier to show you than try to explain."

We were nearly to the far wall when Zorah stopped and gestured us to look. The... *thing* was hidden way back amongst the machinery. Six feet tall, and gleaming with a thousand silver points of light.

"What the actual fuck?" Leonides asked, staring at it blankly.

I was staring just as hard, and at just as much of a loss. "Is it... some kind of sculpture?"

It certainly could have been. Once you got past the 'what the hell' aspect, it was undeniably beautiful. The shape offered the suggestion of giant bird wings, though the central part was nothing more than an abstract curve. On closer inspection, the entire thing was made up of individual metal quills, further reinforcing the idea of avian flight.

"Why did the Fae smuggle a giant piece of modern art into your building's basement?" I asked slowly, trying and failing to make any sense whatsoever of the situation.

Leonides was frowning at the sculpture as though its existence personally offended him. "Is there magic attached to it?"

I dragged my focus inward, trying to feel out the invisible currents around me. "I mean… I don't think so? I can still kind of feel Dhuinne's magical signature, but it's just sort of… floating around the place in general. It's not coming off the statue. At least, not that I can see."

I gave Zorah a questioning look.

She nodded slowly. "Yeah. Something still feels a bit weird in the atmosphere, but I don't think it's being caused by this."

I reached out a hand, fascinated by the bizarre but beautiful object. Leonides' fingers closed around my wrist, stopping me before I could touch it.

"Best not," he said.

I let my hand drop, and his light grip slipped away, leaving my skin tingling in its wake. "Sorry," I said. "I think it must have some of that weird Fae shininess going on. It's hard to look away from it— though my pendant isn't flaring the way it does when Fae try to influence me directly."

"One of us should call Edward and see if he's got any insight," Zorah said. "I mean, it doesn't seem dangerous, but they obviously dropped it here for a reason."

A thought occurred to me. "Why not call Albigard instead? Wouldn't he be more likely to know what it is?"

"I would, but he doesn't have a cell phone, and Rans will have his turned off so it doesn't get fried while they're in the car together," Zorah answered immediately, making me feel like an idiot. She paused for a few seconds. "Still, I'll text Rans' phone and have him ask Albigard when he gets a chance. He'll probably be stopping every couple of hours so he can step out and check messages."

"Right." I fumbled for the phone Leonides had given me. "I can try calling Edward. Maybe under the circumstances, you two should go upstairs and mesmerize any of the tenants who are still here to get them to leave?"

"Not a bad idea," Zorah said, looking up from her text message. She sent it and shoved her phone back in her pocket. "Guthrie?"

Leonides was walking around the thing, his attention on the pipes and gauges in the area where it was set up.

"Agreed," he said absently. "I'm just trying to figure out—"

A loud pop followed by a hissing sound had all three of us whirling to face the other direction.

"What was that?" I asked nervously.

Leonides strode in the direction from which the sound had come. There was no way to immediately tell what had caused it; not among the confusion of pipes and ducts around us.

"Not sure," he said cautiously. "It almost sounded like…"

Another pop came from a different part of the basement. A third followed seconds later, then a fourth and a fifth. I spun in a circle, trying to get a sense of anything out of place in my unfamiliar surroundings. I drew breath to say something, only to freeze as a faint hint of rotten-egg smell tickled my nose.

"Problem," I said. "Um… guys? Big, *big* problem."

SEVEN

They both turned to look at me, their expressions questioning. It took a beat for me to realize why they hadn't noticed the distinctive smell at the same time I did. Vampires didn't breathe unless they had a reason to.

"Breathe in," I said.

Two more pops followed close on the heels of my words, sounding louder than the others. The smell of rotten eggs grew stronger.

"Gas," Zorah said. "It's the natural gas lines. *Shit...* where's the master cut-off valve? There has to be one, right?"

Pipes around us creaked audibly. I yelped as a much louder explosion came from a heavier section of conduit running along the wall near the weird Fae statue. The smell became choking; my eyes began to burn and water.

Leonides' jaw clenched. "That was a main line. Zorah, get Vonnie to safety. I'll stay here and find the shut-off."

My heart stuttered in fear. Quickly, I reinforced the reflective mirror inside my pendant, not wanting to let any magic sneak past unintentionally that might add to the volatile atmosphere.

"You should come, too!" I said, only to descend into coughing.

Zorah looked decidedly unhappy. "She's right. This place is huge. The gas shouldn't be building up this fast. It's not natural. We all need to get out."

I blinked to clear my streaming eyes, in time to see Leonides shake his head.

"There are still people upstairs, Zorah," he said. "Get her away from here. *Now*. She can barely breathe."

Zorah wavered visibly.

Leonides' eyes snapped fire at her. "I'll be right behind you. *Go!*"

Zorah bit her lip. After a moment's hesitation, her unnaturally strong fingers wrapped around my upper arm and I was being dragged in the direction we'd come, toward the staircase.

"Wait—" I tried, but coughing overcame me again before I could get anything else out.

"I'll get you to safety, and then come back to make sure he gets out okay," Zorah said, seemingly unaffected by the choking atmosphere.

How far away constituted 'safe' when it came to gas main leaks in high-rise buildings? I was absolutely certain I'd seen news stories about leaks like that taking out entire city blocks.

No, I told myself firmly. *Leonides will shut off the main, and it'll be all right. Really, it's a good thing we were down here to see it happen, otherwise it might've had time to build up to truly dangerous levels. It'll be fine.*

It seemed to take twice as long to get back to the stairwell as it had to cross the floor in the first place. Zorah was hurrying, while I stumbled along behind her clumsily. To my tear-blurred eyes, the space in front of us seemed to stretch out like toffee. My lungs burned as I tried to draw breath.

Shouldn't the air be clearer than this, as we got farther away from the gas main?

Finally... *finally*, we reached the stairwell door. Zorah wrenched it open. When it closed behind us, I sucked in a deep breath, able to breathe properly at last. Her fingers still gripped my arm, and she pulled me up the stairs without pausing to let me get my breath back.

"We'll leave through the parking garage," she said tightly. "Hopefully he will have found the shut-off by now —"

Pressure slammed into my eardrums, and the world shifted sideways beneath my stumbling feet. The explosion was too big for my senses to properly register it as noise. My shins barked painfully against the edge of the steps as I went down hard, unable to keep my footing as the building moved around me.

The door below us — the one we'd come through moments before — blew off its hinges. Somehow, Zorah was on top of me, her body pressing full length over my back as a blast of heat and flames whooshed past us through the stairwell. It prickled across the small hairs on my arms and the back of my hands, making it feel as though the skin was pulling tight. The smell of scorched fabric and hair tickled my nose.

I coughed and wheezed, trying to gain enough space to breathe beneath the hard weight pinning me. The world had at least stopped sliding sideways, I realized a moment later. That was good, right?

"Talk to me, Von." Zorah's voice sounded like it was coming to me underwater. "You with me?"

I swallowed several times, making an attempt to take stock. "M'okay," I managed thickly, barely able to hear myself. "You…?"

"Vampire, remember?" she said, the words still sounding distant and attenuated. "I'm burned, but healing… although these clothes may never be the same, and my hairstylist is probably going to kill me. The hair will grow back soon enough, but my roots are gonna be a mess."

Her weight lifted from my back, and I grunted as she pulled me upright on shaky legs. The lights were out. I was pretty sure the step I was standing on was now at an angle. Something horrible occurred to me, and I turned, trying to stumble back down the stairs in the dark.

"Leonides!" I gasped, tugging at the grip on my arm when it brought me up short.

"No. We're not thinking about that right now," Zorah said, something hard as nails behind her voice. "We're getting you out of here safely, *after* which I'll fly back in and find him. He's a vampire, too, Vonnie. I told you, vampires are tough. But you're human."

I jerked against her hold again, panic swirling the air around me for a moment until I dragged my magic under control. Her fingers didn't budge.

"But—" I rasped.

"But nothing. The faster you move, the faster I can get back here and make sure he's all right. Now *come on!*"

It was fairly apparent that if I didn't move my feet in the direction Zorah was pulling me, she'd drag me along behind her by brute force. None of the steps were where my feet expected to encounter them. Everything was an inch too high or an inch too low, and at one point I gasped when the step I expected wasn't there at all, which immediately made me start coughing again.

Through it all, Zorah's grip on me was like iron. The concrete of the next landing had apparently cracked in two — one half had heaved upward several inches, lying on a slant. I discovered this by virtue of stubbing my toe on the lip, releasing another pained yelp in the process.

I needed Edward's glowing flashlight magic, damn it. As soon as the thought registered, I cursed myself and reached for my back pocket, where — thankfully — the burner phone still nestled, hopefully undamaged. Pulling it out, I fumbled the power button on and pulled down the flashlight app from the menu at the top. White light swung crazily around the landing, illuminating huge, spidering cracks in the concrete wall. The door was jammed at an odd angle in its twisted frame. Dust filtered down on our heads in gray swirls.

"Stand back," Zorah said through gritted teeth, finally letting me go in favor of grabbing the door handle in both hands. She set her feet and wrenched the door inward with an awful screech of metal. It opened maybe eight or nine inches before the bottom ground to a halt against the slanted concrete floor. Another wrench gained another couple of inches, the metal door bowing in the middle.

"Go, *go*," she snapped.

I scrambled over the broken floor and breathed out, making myself as small as possible so I could squeeze through the gap sideways. The choking dust was worse in the parking garage, with even more sprinkling down on us as an ominous groan of strain rumbled through the eight-story mass of steel and concrete above us.

I played the flashlight over the area in front of us, revealing more chunks of floor jutting up like icebergs. Parts of the floor were gone completely, collapsed into the underground level we'd just come from. Steam from the machinery in the basement wafted up through some of the holes, joining with the trickles of disintegrating concrete from the ceiling. Smoke and flames were visible through other gaps.

A panicked sob caught in my chest, as I thought of Leonides—possibly trapped down there. I swallowed roughly to keep the sound from escaping. The parking garage's only entrance was on the far end of the building from where we'd emerged. Because *of course* it fucking was. My flashlight couldn't reach nearly that far, but a faint glow of daylight filtered to us from that direction, made murky by the haze of dust and steam.

"Hurry," Zorah said. "Watch your footing."

She took my free hand this time, rather than my arm. Despite her exhortation to hurry, we had to pick our way carefully across the space. Of course, Zorah could have flown and been out in moments, but one wrong step for me and I'd end up falling into the burning disaster area below us.

Another tortured groan came from the building's structure. Zorah dragged me sideways as a chunk of concrete two feet across crashed down from the ceiling. My heart raced as the building's groan became a bone-shaking rumble, and the floor beneath me started to slide sideways again.

"Shit shit *shit!*" Zorah cursed, her voice rising in pitch as she yanked me toward the nearest stretch of wall, where angular support beams stood every few feet like sentinels.

I stumbled over debris, more chunks of ceiling falling around us as the rumble grew into a deafening roar. Zorah slammed me against the wall in the space next to a jutting beam. A hand on my shoulder forced me into a crouch, as her body once again covered mine in a tense arch.

"Hold on!" she shouted, as everything began to shake and shudder around us. The air grew even more choked with dust and smoke. I cradled the useless phone to my stomach, the flashlight illuminating only impenetrable gray.

The roar of the disintegrating building rose to a crescendo, and everything went black as the world fell on our heads.

Pain woke me.

I moaned, trying to curl toward the agony burning in my left arm and shoulder. Pressure on my other shoulder kept me in place.

"Vonnie? *Vonnie!*" The voice echoed painfully through my aching head.

Another groan emerged from my throat. My tongue felt like I'd tried to swallow dry flour — powdery and disgusting. I tried to open my eyes and whimpered, because they, too, were covered with a coating of clinging dust.

The hand on my shoulder squeezed. "No, keep your eyes closed. Just breathe for a minute."

Distantly, I heard a sound like boulders sliding down a mountain, and the hard concrete at my back shook.

"The building's not stable," said the voice. "*Shit*, I hope this slab holds…"

Flickers of memory started to filter in. *Zorah.* Zorah was with me. We'd been trying to get out of the building before… before…

"Hold still," she said grimly. "I'm going to get some of this dust off your face so you can open your eyes. Believe it or not, the damn phone survived, so there's light — for all the good it does us right now."

Something soft brushed lightly across my face… cloth, I thought — perhaps a sleeve or the hem of a shirt. When it moved away, I turned my head to the side and spit, trying to call more saliva to my mouth as some of the feeling of choking on dust faded to tolerable levels.

"We're in an airspace," Zorah said. "But your arm is trapped under rubble. I'm going to pull it off you now, but it's likely to hurt like a bitch, and I don't know what shape the arm is in beneath it. I'm really sorry, hon."

I nodded my understanding, only to gasp when the tiny movement jarred my shoulder. "Okay," I whispered weakly.

I kept my eyes closed, not quite ready to make our situation more real than it already was. Something heavy shifted across my arm and shoulder before rolling away. Another piece of rubble followed… and another… and another.

Perversely, the pain grew worse once the heavy pressure trapping the limb was gone. I couldn't stop a high-pitched keening noise from slipping free of my throat, as the dull agony from before grew razor-sharp talons and started tearing at me.

"Fuck," Zorah cursed. "Jesus fuck, that's bad."

I dragged my fraying control together, still not daring to look. "You're terrible at this!" I managed in a wavering voice. "You're supposed to tell me it'll be fine!"

Her hand cupped the side of my neck and jaw, comforting. "Sorry, Von. Of course it'll be fine. You're going to have some nice demon-laced vampire blood, and it's going to heal. And then we're going to figure out how to get you out of here."

With a jolt, it began to truly sink in that Leonides' building had just collapsed. The Vixen's Den… the Brown Fox… it was gone, or at least heavily damaged. The penthouse… the bed I'd set on fire… the kitchen where Len made his amazing tapas…

And Leonides had been in the basement when the gas leak ignited.

"Oh my god. He's dead, isn't he?" I asked in a tiny, quavering whisper.

Zorah didn't pretend not to know what I was talking about. "No, babe. He's not dead; he's a vampire. He'll heal and get out just fine. It doesn't take much of a gap for mist to fly through. Let's just worry about us, okay?"

My body was starting to tremble, shock setting in as the pain from my shattered arm took its toll. "Y-you could fly out, too. G-go get help."

"Not just yet," she said. Cool skin brushed my lips, dripping wet with something salty. "I need you to swallow as much of this as you can for me, sweetheart. Okay?"

It was blood. I closed my lips over Zorah's wrist without thought, trying not to choke on the coppery liquid as it dripped into my mouth. My tongue encountered the edges of the deep gash she'd made in her own flesh. I could feel the wound closing even as I sucked and swallowed. The blood stopped flowing, and she pulled it away, only to return it a moment later with a fresh slash from her fangs.

I kept drinking, because the alternative was to be injured and helpless in this claustrophobic air-space underneath a collapsed high-rise. Already, I could feel the beginnings of a jittery buzz spreading outward from my stomach—tingling warmth. The tingles reached my injured arm and I arched away from her, crying out with something that wasn't... *quite*... pain.

"Easy," Zorah soothed, steadying me by my other shoulder. "You'll be okay in a few minutes— hang in there."

I panted shallowly, trying to avoid pulling more of the floating dust into my lungs. Where I was hurt, I could feel the familiar itch of forced healing spreading beneath my skin... burrowing deep through bone and sinew. Elsewhere, though, the power from Zorah's blood danced across my nerves like hot fingers, stroking. I squirmed, feeling my nipples harden to points beneath my bra.

Her thumb stroked soothing circles on my shoulder, but 'soothed' was pretty much the opposite of what I was feeling.

"This feels different than last time," I said with a gasp. "Why is it different?"

I couldn't help a small note of hysteria from creeping into my voice. It also seemed to be taking a lot longer than when Rans had given me his blood, after I'd been shot. My eyes flew open as something in my arm snapped painfully into place, and I finally took a good look at our surroundings in the wavering beam of the phone's flashlight LED.

I got a confused impression of concrete angled above us like the sloping wall of an attic—maybe part of the roof that had fallen and lodged against the wall where we'd huddled for safety. Piles of rubble surrounded us, and the whole space was barely more than five feet by five feet.

"Try to stay calm, hon," Zorah said, with admirable steadiness. "I'm still just a baby vamp—not like Rans. I'm also a demon, and there's Fae magic mixed up in my blood, too. Though I imagine it's mostly the demon part that you're feeling. It's got kind of a predictable effect on people, unfortunately."

Cartilage crackled alarmingly in my shoulder. I resolutely *did not look*.

"What kind of effect?" The hysterical quaver was still there. I shifted in place again, my skin feeling overheated and sensitive.

There was a beat of silence, broken only by the sound of the building shifting.

"I'm one-quarter succubus, Vonnie," Zorah said flatly. "My blood makes people horny. Nigellus basically called it undead Viagra. So... um. Sorry about that. The good news is, it's not permanent or anything. It'll go away eventually."

I took a moment to try and process that, failed, and put it aside — barely managing to stifle a shriek as my elbow twisted sharply into place, and the itching grew in intensity.

"Okay, cool," I managed in a pained squeak.

In the absence of alternatives, I rode out the next few minutes with gritted teeth and extremely erect nipples, until the unpleasant buzzing in my arm faded to tolerable levels. My bruised shins were already healed, and the general air of having been put through a clothes-wringer was replaced with the feeling of unnatural vitality I'd begun to grow accustomed to after drinking Leonides' blood.

If anything, I felt like meth users must, after that first, addictive hit.

This is your brain on succubus blood, I thought nonsensically, gathering the courage to look down at my arm and assess the state of it. It was covered with blood, and that blood was caked with dust. But when I cautiously wiggled my fingers, nothing horrible happened. The deep itch danced along the muscles at first, but it grew less and less noticeable as I carefully moved first my wrist, then my elbow, and finally my shoulder.

"All fixed now?" Zorah asked, most of her attention on our claustrophobic surroundings.

"Yeah," I breathed, knowing I should be used to this kind of thing after the past few crazy weeks. After Ivan's goons kneecapping me... after the SWAT team shooting Edward, what was a tiny little shattered arm between friends? I absolutely was not going to mention the way my belly throbbed, low and insistent, or the unusual fullness and sensitivity between my legs.

God — did normal women deal with this kind of shit *all the time*? If so, it was really, *really* distracting.

"Okay," Zorah said. "Next order of business — getting the hell out of here. I'm going to have to leave you for a few minutes so I can figure out where we are in relation to the outside world. I swear I'll be right back as soon as I get the layout, though. Do you trust me, Von?"

"I trust you, Zorah," I told her. "But you should still find Leonides first."

"I'll make a quick sweep outside. If he's not there, it'll have to wait until after we get you out," she insisted. "Now, hang tight. And you should probably check the battery on the phone. Turn the light off if it's getting low."

I nodded.

"I'll be back," she repeated, before dissipating into vapor that mixed with the swirling dust motes and disappearing.

Leaving me alone.

EIGHT

I stared blankly at the cracked concrete slab sheltering the small space, feeling my heart thudding
a rapid beat inside my chest. It took me several
moments to pull my gaze away from the flimsy
barrier separating me from a mountain of crushing
rubble.

The phone battery was still at eighty percent. I
made an executive decision to leave the flashlight
app on, knowing it would be much harder to keep
my shit together in pitch-black surroundings.

Jesus. We hadn't even needed to discuss using
it to call 911. Not with the Fae involved. At best, it
would be a waste of time. At worst, it would be like
waving a big sign that said, 'Hey, we're not dead
yet—come take another shot while you have the
chance!'

I propped the phone on my lap, squirming in a
fruitless attempt to relieve the throb between my
legs. My hand rose to my pendant—an uncon-
scious gesture of self-soothing. Once I touched the
smooth crystal, it occurred to me to look inward, in
hopes of seeing if there was anything obviously
magical still going on around me. I had a pretty
good idea that those gas pipes hadn't spontane-
ously failed due to natural causes. As traps went,

though, it honestly seemed like a bizarre choice, especially for a couple of vampires.

That was a bad direction to let my thoughts turn, because thinking about vampires meant thinking about Leonides caught in the hellscape of the gas explosion on the floor below. I wrenched my attention back to the crystal and let my senses flow outward through the focus, searching.

Nothing. I couldn't even feel the nebulous magical miasma from earlier. Everything was just... normal.

Yeah, said the hysterical little voice in my head. *Totally normal day, here. Nothing out of the ordinary at all...*

Zorah would be back soon. I repeated that to myself aloud a couple of times, for emphasis. But then what? I was in a five-foot by five-foot space with no doors or windows; an avalanche poised above me, ready to randomly come crashing down at any moment.

Sweat broke out on my forehead, my pulse speeding further.

Maybe Zorah thought she could tear through the rubble with the same supernatural strength she'd used to force the heavy metal door open and lift chunks of concrete off me. Was that plausible? I wasn't sure. We'd still been a long way from the entrance to the parking garage when the building collapsed. That entrance might not even exist anymore. There could be a solid mountain of rubble between here and the way out.

Fear shuddered through me, the emotion escaping my control and whipping up the dust in the small space as the air swirled. I quickly focused on containing my power, taken by surprise at the strength of the magical reaction.

Christ. Zorah's blood must be hitting me even harder than Leonides' did, at least in the magic department. Was it because of her demon heritage? Or maybe the Fae magic she'd mentioned? A combination?

And then, it hit me. I was surrounded by air and stone—or rather, concrete. But concrete was just cement, crushed rock, and water mixed together, right? And I sucked at lithomancy in the general course of things, but I'd just drunk vampire blood, and I was *really* motivated right now.

Cautiously, I let my thoughts turn toward the ever-present ache of sadness I felt at Jace's absence, focusing the feeling through the crystal and aiming it toward one of the chunks of rubble on the floor— a chunk that had my blood staining one sharp edge.

The concrete cracked in two, bits of shrapnel shooting out from the break and peppering me. I flinched, but almost immediately turned the phone's light toward it to confirm what I thought I'd seen. Sure enough, it was the most damage I'd ever managed to do to an earth-based material... and I'd been holding back.

Zorah's hybrid blood was supercharging my magic.

I craned around, examining the relatively undamaged wall at my back. If I was right, this was an exterior wall—the one that faced east, I was pretty sure. A crazy idea began to percolate through my brain. Just then, cool fog swirled into the cramped space, and I turned in time to see Zorah's slender form spiral into existence in front of me.

"Did you find him?" I asked immediately.

Fresh worry pinched her expression. "No, he wasn't outside… at least, not in the immediate vicinity. It's bad out there, Von. About a quarter of the building just kind of sheared off and collapsed. More could go any time. We need to get you out of here before it does. There's some good news, though."

I swallowed another sarcastic quip in response, because Zorah probably couldn't help being bad at reassurance.

"Okay. What's the good news?" I asked instead.

She looked at the wall above my head. "The parking level isn't completely below-grade, and if I'm right, the top of this wall is at street level. I just have to figure out how to get through it without bringing everything on top of us crashing down."

"Wait, are you sure about that?" I pressed, trying to remember details of the building that I'd never really paid much attention to in the normal course of things. This whole block was on a slight hill—nothing major, but it meant that the entrance to the 'underground' parking garage was, in fact, at street level. There was a ramp going down as you drove in… but it wasn't very steep.

Zorah nodded. "Pretty sure, yeah. I found the right stretch of wall and listened for your heartbeat to figure out where you were in relation to the level of the sidewalk."

I took a deep, steadying breath, and regretted it immediately when I started coughing.

"Right," I rasped, once I'd recovered enough to speak. "I want you to point out exactly where I need to break through. Then I want you to shift into mist and stay out of the way."

"Where *you* need to break through?" Zorah echoed blankly. "No offense, but I kind of figured I'd be the one doing the demolition work."

I shook my head. "Nope. Not this time. I'm an elemental witch, and I'm surrounded by air and concrete with tiny rocks in it. So stand back and let me do my thing."

She still looked unconvinced. "With magic? Are you sure you're strong enough?"

I scowled. "Let's just say vampire-succubus blood is inspiring in more ways than one."

She paused for only a beat before nodding her acceptance, and I loved her just a little bit more in that moment.

"Okay, babe. Let's do this thing." She stretched her arm up, indicating an area close to the jutting support beam that still appeared relatively undamaged—and which would hopefully prevent further collapse when the wall crumbled. "If you can make a hole right about here, I'll fly through, rematerialize, and pull you out."

Right. If you can even do this in the first place, prodded an irritating voice of self-doubt.

I ignored it.

"Got it," I told her. "Now — stop being so corporeal, and stay behind me. There's about to be a very big blast of wind in a very small space. I've got a feeling this isn't going to be pretty."

Zorah squeezed my shoulder as I climbed to my feet and turned to face the outer wall. "You go, girl," she said. A moment later, the grip of fingers dissolved away to nothing.

My body was still buzzing with frustrated energy. I focused fixedly on the small patch of wall — first with my eyes, and then with my inner awareness of magical fields. Rock and air. Sadness and fear.

Looking inward, I unchained the elephant in the room… the thing I'd been refusing to think about too closely, because if I thought about it, I'd start screaming and maybe not be able to stop.

Leonides had been standing at ground zero of a natural gas explosion that had torn the front off an eight-story building. He wasn't outside when Zorah did a sweep around the block to look for him. Nor was he here, swooping in to the rescue — my knight in tarnished armor.

No matter what Zorah had said to try and keep me calm earlier, it was very possible that the man who'd saved me from Ivan — who'd sheltered me from the madness of Dhuinne and touched me with the kind of reverence and consideration no man had ever shown me before — was trapped in an inferno with his flesh burning from his bones.

The fire would keep raging until someone managed to cut off the gas flow from outside. Even here, halfway across the length of the destroyed building, I could smell smoke. Leonides was in a fire right now, suffering the most agonizing pain imaginable.

My body began to shake.

A human would die under those conditions, but if Zorah was to be believed, a vampire... *wouldn't*. He would just keep burning.

This man had bled for me. He'd been *shot in the neck* for me, and he'd waved it away as if it was nothing. He'd never wanted to be a vampire. He'd just wanted Rans to let him go; wanted to be free of his long, bleak life of servitude to a demon. He'd wanted to die, and now he couldn't. Not from a fire. Not from a collapsing building.

My knees wobbled and gave way. I fell to the hard floor, focusing every iota of this feeling at the section of wall above me as a wavering cry of grief and terror for the man who'd done nothing but protect me wrenched free of my throat. The sound grew into a scream—a wordless protest against the injustice of it all. The idea that I might never see him again settled over me like a pall... followed closely by the idea that I *would*, but that this experience might have broken him, in body or mind or both.

Grief poured through the pendant, sharp and inescapable. The concrete wall erupted in a spider web of deep cracks, small chunks pattering down to land at my feet. I unleashed all of my considerable fear an instant later, and the mosaic of broken pieces exploded outward beneath the tightly focused magical blast.

I remained crouched on my knees, panting and crying. The air cleared gradually, revealing an uneven hole maybe two feet wide, just beneath the slab of collapsed roof that defined the ceiling of the cramped space. Still choking on dust and sobs, I staggered to my feet. The cloud of fog that was Zorah whooshed through the new opening.

A moment later, slender fingers closed around a broken edge of concrete and ripped it away — widening the gap into something a person might reasonably be able to squeeze through. Above me, rubble shifted, grinding like boulders. One edge of the protective slab slid downward an inch or two, gritty dust falling through the tiny gap like rain.

Zorah's head and shoulders appeared through the hole I'd just blasted. If the slab gave way while she was in that position, it would tear her body in half. My unsteady breath caught in my throat as she reached down with both hands.

"I don't much like the sound of that rubble grinding together," she said urgently. "Come on!"

I grabbed hold of her wrists with shaking fingers, not at all sure I had the strength left to haul myself up. Thirty years old, and I'd never done a single pull-up or chin-up in my life. While it was true I'd also never been this motivated before, I was still weak with reaction after unleashing the most powerful double-blast of magic I'd ever managed to channel.

Zorah's iron grip closed around my wrists in return. "Walk up the wall with your feet until I can pull your upper body through," she ordered, and suddenly it didn't matter how strong my biceps were, because I was being hoisted off the ground.

I scrambled to get my feet against the wall as she pulled me up, seemingly without effort. The newly healed muscle and sinew in my crushed arm strained, but held. The rough edges of the hole scraped against my flesh with bruising force as my head, shoulders, and chest slid through the gap. My legs flailed, and I barely managed to contain a fresh flare of panic as I realized I was now the one poised to have my spine snapped in half if the ceiling slab gave way.

My hips jammed against the edges of the hole for an awful moment before Zorah wrenched me the rest of the way through. My body popped free of the opening like a champagne cork, and suddenly I was lying face down on a chilly sidewalk. Grit and bits of broken concrete ground against my cheek as I coughed and gasped, tears still running down my filthy face.

"Up," Zorah insisted, hauling me off the ground by the grip she still held on my wrists. "Move... *move!*"

My legs didn't want to obey my brain's commands, but she hauled my right arm over her shoulders and started walking. There was no choice but to follow. Out here, the sound of the building's structure giving up its slow-motion fight against gravity sounded somehow more immediate. Dazed, I craned around to look, but my brain struggled to put the confused images in context.

Leonides' building... wasn't a building anymore. And he was still inside.

NINE

One side of the high-rise had collapsed, like a sandcastle after an angry child had poured a bucket of water over it. Massive cracks riddled what was left, and the pieces no longer fit together properly. Ninety-degree angles were subtly off; there were gaps in the facade where there definitely shouldn't be gaps. Smoke poured from the side with the worst damage.

I tripped over my own feet, and a sharp tug from Zorah got me looking where I was going again, instead of staring behind me. Distantly, I registered the sounds of screaming bystanders and sirens. Zorah ignored it all as she frog-marched me across the street and down the block. She didn't stop until we'd put another full block between us and the disaster zone, our view of the structure blocked by a building just as large, but undamaged.

I moved my feet, one in front of the other — aware of a growing crowd of people milling around. Zorah dragged me into a deserted alley and set my back against the wall for support.

"You have to go find him, Zorah!" I told her, more than a bit hysterically, grabbing her shoulders and squeezing with trembling fingers. "Please… he could be burning right now — you have to get him out!"

She nodded, her expression haunted in the light slanting in from the street. "He should have been able to get out on his own," she said, and her voice didn't sound any steadier than mine. "Even with the blast, he should have been able to shift and fly away." She paused, visibly uncertain. "Maybe he went back inside looking for us, instead of staying out here."

I squeezed her shoulders harder — hard enough to bruise, if she'd been human. "Just find him!"

Zorah nodded, worry lighting her brown gaze with molten copper. "Stay here. Hide. Don't let *anyone* see you. I'll be as quick as I can."

She thought the Fae would be coming soon, to make sure the job was finished. The Fae... or their operatives. Suddenly, the sirens converging on the collapsed building took on a much more sinister aspect.

"Hurry," I told her. "I'll be all right."

She left.

Spoiler alert — I was not remotely all right.

Using a hand on the wall to brace myself, I stumbled to the end of the alley and managed a semi-controlled collapse into a tiny space behind a collection of trashcans. The asphalt beneath my butt was sticky with god-knew-what, and the smell from the trashcans was sickening. My entire body was coated with gray dust, darker in the places where it mixed with drying blood. I pulled the phone out of my pocket. The flashlight app was still on, so I turned it off. The battery was down to sixty-eight percent.

Blessedly, my mind settled into the soft blankness of shock. The sound of people on the street beyond my smelly haven gradually quieted. The authorities must have been moving everyone out of the area—establishing a safety perimeter.

I had no idea how long I sat there, but the angle of the light slanting in from the alley mouth was noticeably deeper when the approach of scuffing footsteps broke through my shell of numbness. Holding my breath, I waited to see if they would go past or turn into the alley. The footsteps entered without hesitation, heading straight for my hiding place. I scrambled to my feet. Either it was Zorah, who already knew I was here and could sense my location from the sound of my heartbeat... or the Fae had found me somehow. Either way, I'd be better off upright.

My relief on seeing Zorah's slender form evaporated abruptly as my overwrought brain registered the shape sprawled over her shoulder in a fireman's carry. A gasp escaped me, and it wasn't because of the impossibility of someone as slender as her carrying something so large and heavy. I caught myself with a hand braced on the lid of the trashcan next to me, my vision wavering in and out of focus.

I will not faint... I will not faint... I silently repeated the words a few times, forcing myself to take slow, deep breaths. The smell of burned flesh tickled my nose, competing with the stench of trash.

The figure could only be Leonides—who else would Zorah be carrying through the streets, her face looking as though she was about a second away from losing her shit and collapsing into hysterics?

Just as the building we'd escaped wasn't really a building anymore, the body slung over Zorah's small frame wasn't a person anymore. What rags of clothing were left had melted into bubbling flesh. His hair was gone. His… *skin* was gone. What had been rich umber was now a mosaic of crimson and black that my mind refused to make sense of.

"Vonnie…" Zorah's voice emerged small and quavering. "He's… he's not healing…"

The badass demon-vampire who'd quipped her way through a building falling on us sounded suddenly, *desperately* young as she supported her grandfather's horrifically burned body. Something shifted in my consciousness, sliding sideways into a kind of strangely detached maternal survival mode. The numbness was back, but paired now with an absolute, iron will to get us out of here, to somewhere safe where we could lick our wounds and consider our next steps.

I locked my knees and stepped away from the support of the trashcan.

"*Zorah*," I said sharply. "Talk to me. Is he dead, or can he still come back from this?"

Her chest shuddered. "I… I don't…" She swallowed hard, making a visible effort to pull herself together. "His head's still attached and he hasn't been staked. Those are supposed to be the only ways to kill a vampire."

"But?" I prompted, sensing there was more.

"I pulled two dozen silver quills out of his body after I got him out. That statue thing in the basement—it was a shrapnel bomb. Only, one made specifically for vampires. It blew apart when the gas main exploded. He must've been standing right there. It's why he couldn't shift into mist and fly away."

"Okay," I said, still in my 'crisis management' voice. Still detached from the horror that was right in front of me. "We need to go someplace safe. I'm guessing we can't take him to a hospital? And the Fae know where I live. So... a hotel. You can mesmerize someone into giving us a car so we can get there. We'll try calling Rans again—he'll know what to do next. Do you have cash, and your phone?"

Her clothing was badly scorched, though not burned completely away—and while her skin was smoke-blackened, she appeared otherwise unmarked.

"I don't know," she said, still sounding lost and out of her depth. "I don't want to put him down to check."

"It doesn't matter," I decided. "You can influence the hotel desk clerk if we need to, and we'll worry about your phone later. Mine's okay. Come on—we're going. Straight to the nearest road that still has traffic on it."

She nodded—a hint of her usual composure returning, though it looked decidedly frayed. I could only imagine what this was going to look like to anyone who saw us. Me, covered in dust and blood; Zorah with her burned clothing and grisly burden. I resolved not to worry about it. There would be plenty of sensationalism to go around on the TV news today. We were just one small piece of that.

I led the way out of the alley and got my bearings, heading for the road where I sometimes used to park for my shifts at the club. It was quiet but not deserted on most nights, and would hopefully yield up a van or SUV or something we could use, without also subjecting us to the attention of dozens of other drivers whizzing past.

A pair of EMTs hauling medical bags came jogging toward us, speeding up when they caught sight of Leonides. "*Jesus!*" One of them said as they slid to a halt. "Ma'am, put him down, please. We're medical professionals, we can—"

Zorah's eyes blazed, her lip curling up to reveal sharp fangs. "Keep going! You didn't see us," she hissed, and started walking again. I glanced over my shoulder as the blank-faced EMTs began heading calmly in the other direction.

A pair of cops manning a barricade at the next intersection got a similar treatment, and then we were outside the perimeter. I made an executive decision, turning to Zorah and indicating a recessed entryway in a nearby building.

"Wait over there," I told her. "I'll flag down something big enough for us to use, and keep them talking until you can come over and flash the vampire high-beams at them."

She nodded, still atypically compliant. I positioned myself behind one of the large trees lining the sidewalk, where it wouldn't be quite as obvious what a mess I was to anyone casually driving past. The first few vehicles to go by were sedans and coupes, too small for what I needed. Drivers were rubbernecking, slowing down to try and see what was happening three blocks over. At least that meant they were too distracted to notice me, lurking bloody and dust-covered behind a tree, or Zorah with her grim burden in the shadow of a doorway.

Finally, a late model mini-van turned onto the street. Ignoring my growing shakiness, I waited until it was a few hundred feet away and stepped into the lane, raising my hand in an imperious 'stop' gesture. Brakes squealed, and the minivan came to a stop maybe thirty feet away from me. I hurried toward it, seeing the driver's wide-eyed expression through the windshield.

"Please!" I called, putting a hand on the hood to discourage the woman from driving around me and taking off as fast as she could. "I need help — there's been an explosion!"

Cautiously, she rolled down the driver's side window and stuck her head out. "Are you hurt? Do you need me to call 911?"

"Yeah… I really wish it were that easy," I said, as Zorah jogged up, Leonides still slung improbably across her shoulders.

The driver opened her mouth — probably to scream bloody murder — but Zorah's gaze was already pinning her.

"Quiet," Zorah said. "In a minute, you're going to pick up your purse and phone, and step out of the vehicle. Leave the van key in the ignition and the motor running. Take your other keys. There was a high-rise collapse, and you let some people use your vehicle to take an injured guy to the hospital. You didn't think to get their names; you just said yes, because it was the right thing to do. You're not going to report the van stolen for a few days. You know it was for a good cause."

The woman nodded vacantly and reached across to get her bag from the passenger seat. We stepped out of the way as she opened the door and got out, her gaze sliding over Leonides' burned body as though it didn't even register. I watched her walk away, only to jerk my attention back to the road when another car turned onto the street a couple blocks north of us.

"Hurry," I said, pushing the unlock button on the driver's door. "I'll drive."

Zorah opened the sliding side door and eased Leonides to lie full-length along the rear bench seat. I hopped into the driver's seat and adjusted it, still feeling utterly removed from what I was doing and what was going on around me. Zorah slammed the side door shut from inside, and I put the vehicle in drive before hitting the gas pedal.

Fumbling one-handed in my pocket, I pulled out my phone and handed it back to Zorah. "Find me one of those cheap, one-story motels where you park right in front of the door to the room," I ordered. "Somewhere close, but not *too* close. Try searching for 'motor lodge' rather than hotel. In East St. Louis, maybe."

"Okay," she said shakily.

I wasn't sure how much I should be worrying about the Fae coming after us, but there was no point in making things easy for them. Besides, I doubted there were any motels like the kind I was thinking of in the immediate area. This part of the city was too gentrified. I headed toward the interstate and took the eastbound exit, figuring that if our backup was likely to be coming from Chicago, we might as well be across the river in Illinois.

There would be plenty of cheap roadside motels on the other side of the Mississippi.

"Got one," Zorah said. "It's in Alorton. Take I-64 across the river, then get on Highway 15 going south. The Dee-Luxe Motel is at the Pocket Road exit."

I nodded, fixing the directions in my memory.

"How is he?" I asked against my better judgment. At least I managed to stop myself from trying to catch a glimpse of the body in the rearview mirror.

"The same," Zorah said, the tremor back in her voice.

I nodded. "Try calling Rans again. Did your phone make it?"

There was a brief pause. Then, "No, it's toast."

"Use mine," I said. "I'm guessing he won't have that number, so maybe a voice message? That way he'll know it's really you, and not some kind of a trick."

"Yeah," she said thickly. Another pause, as she dialed from memory and waited for voicemail to pick up. "Lover? It's me. Please check your damned messages soon. We need help. G's hurt bad, and he's not healing. Tinkerbell knows how to find us, and I need you to get here fast, okay?"

From her tone of voice, Rans would have no doubt that this was serious, because Zorah was clearly freaking out. But at least she was still holding it together well enough that she hadn't slipped and used Albigard's or Leonides' names, which was probably more than I'd have managed in her place.

I cursed the vagaries of Fae magic that prevented Rans from getting the message right away. I wasn't even sure how long it had been since Zorah had texted him about the weird silver shrapnel-statue in the basement. Two hours, maybe? It seemed like a decade.

We drove in silence, crossing the Poplar Street Bridge — the river flowing wide and gray and sluggish beneath us. *So much for vampires not being able to cross running water*, I thought absently.

Eventually, I pulled into the seedy motel's parking lot and brought the van to a halt next to the main office, meeting Zorah's eyes in the mirror. "You're going to have to do this part," I told her. "Whoever's behind the desk is gonna lose it the moment they see any of us. We both look like a burning building fell on us."

She nodded heavily and eased out of the van, trudging toward the office door. I sat with my hands at ten-o'clock and two-o'clock on the wheel, trying desperately not to think about the maybe-dead-maybe-not body of a man for whom I cared deeply, sprawled across the back seat like some kind of grotesque mannequin.

A few minutes later, Zorah returned with an old-fashioned metal key; no fancy-schmancy electronic locks for the Dee-Luxe Motel, apparently. She got in and directed me to room 17, where I parked the van and sat unmoving, suddenly at a loss now that we'd gotten this far.

"It's almost dusk," Zorah said. "Go on inside. I'll bring him in as soon as it's dark enough that no one will notice."

I nodded, pulling myself out of my reverie long enough to look around the lot. There were only three other cars, none of them parked very close. "Okay."

She handed me the phone and the room key. I stepped out of the van on rubbery legs. The lock on the room's door felt loose and jiggly when I twisted the key, but the knob itself jammed. It refused to turn until I yanked upward and jerked the door back and forth at the same time. Finally, it creaked open. I flipped on the lights and looked around, deciding that it looked like a great place to be murdered by a serial killer, or possibly to catch an STD.

It had been a while since I'd seen this much beige in one place.

But none of that mattered. All that mattered was that no one would come looking for us here, and we could hole up until the paranormal cavalry arrived. And then…

My mind did the sliding sideways thing again. The sound of the door opening brought me back to awareness with a gasp. While I'd stood staring at the room in a fugue state, the last of the light had faded outside. Zorah had Leonides draped over her shoulders again. She eased him carefully through the gap, scooting through sideways so they would both fit.

"Lock the door," she said, and her voice sounded like she'd been crying. Maybe she had been, sitting alone with her grandfather in the van. "Grab a pillow and bring it into the bathroom."

I backed into the space between the two double beds to get out of her way, and then did as she asked—too numb to even ask about the purpose of the pillow. The bathroom was dire, but at least someone appeared to have cleaned the white, pink, and mint-green-tiled space on a somewhat regular basis. Even so, the room smelled noticeably of mildew… probably from the shower curtain.

Zorah shoved the offending sheet of plastic out of the way and took the pillow from my slack grip. She tossed it against the end of the tub opposite the spout and lowered Leonides' body into the chipped ceramic basin, resting his head on it.

In the unforgiving fluorescent lighting, my mind came dangerously close to taking in the true extent of his injuries before it snapped abruptly back into dissociation. I looked away, feeling lightheaded.

"What do we do now?" I asked in a monotone.

Zorah looked just as lost as I felt.

The phone buzzed. I nearly fumbled it in my hurry to get it out of my pocket.

"Hello?" I said, a bit desperately.

"*Zorah?*" a British voice demanded at the same time, speaking over me in haste.

"It's Vonnie," I said stupidly. "Zorah's right here."

She grabbed the phone from my hand and lifted it to her ear. "Rans? We need help!"

I couldn't hear the reply, but Zorah said, "No, we're at a motel. No one's around. Okay. Please hurry." Her voice wavered on the final words. She disconnected the call and handed me the phone. "Turn the power off. They'll be here in five minutes."

I took it mechanically and did as she asked. It took me most of the five minutes to realize that Albigard must have recovered enough to bring Rans here with a portal, and his presence would fry the phone if it was still turned on when they arrived.

We didn't speak as the minutes ticked by. Zorah stared fixedly at the body in the tub. I, in turn, stared fixedly at her, to *avoid* seeing the body in the tub.

Energy crackled outside the bathroom door, a brighter light briefly overpowering the fluorescent bulbs over the sink before it faded. Zorah made a desperate noise in the back of her throat and rushed past me. I turned more slowly, just in time to see her barrel into Rans with her full weight. He caught her easily, sweeping her against him and wrapping both arms around her tightly.

"I've got you, love," he murmured, and something inside my chest twisted painfully, cutting off my breath. "It's going to be all right."

TEN

The only person to whom I might conceivably run for comfort in such a way was currently lying in a bathtub, burned beyond all recognition. A choked sob tried to claw its way up my throat. I swallowed it back ruthlessly. Doing so was physically painful.

Albigard sauntered through the fiery portal, still looking pale and gaunt. It snapped shut behind him. His eyes played over the pair of lovers with as much disgust as if he'd walked in on them doing the horizontal mambo, rather than merely embracing each other. His lips twisted in distaste, but rather than say anything, he turned to me. I was still standing in the doorway to the bathroom. The Fae's nostrils flared, scenting the air, and he crossed the room, setting me aside gently with one hand so he could enter.

I watched him approach the bathtub and look down, his shoulders a rigid line. The low voices from the other room went quiet. Then Rans slipped past me as well, moving like a shadow. Standing side by side, the two men took up most of the available space—not that I was in a hurry to join them in looking down at the body in the tub.

Zorah approached to hover behind my shoulder. Rans turned away from the grisly sight first, his classically handsome face set into hard lines.

"Let's get him someplace warded, so we can be relatively confident we won't be found," he said. "Zorah, you can raid a blood bank in Chicago and get some bagged blood for him. Then, we'll see what can be done. From what you've described, it's possible there's still silver inside him — that might explain why he's not regenerating properly."

Albigard turned and raised an eyebrow at me. "I will need to draw power from you again to conjure another portal so soon. I am still drained."

I nodded absently. "Yeah. Join the club," I told him. "But I think I know how to fix that."

Rans' glacier-blue gaze fell on me. "Oh?"

I met his eyes. "Turns out, vampire-succubus blood packs even more of a punch than yours does."

He blinked.

"It's true," Zorah confirmed. "She blew out a solid concrete wall to escape from the collapsed building."

Rans continued to stare. After a moment, he seemed to shake himself free of his thoughts. "As long as you're aware of the, erm, *side effects*, so to speak."

"Horniness, yeah, got the memo," I replied in a flat tone. "Not really an issue right now, trust me." I glanced at Zorah. "Give me some more of your blood, please, so we can go."

"Which one of us is the vampire here?" she joked weakly, but she bared fangs and opened a vein for me nonetheless.

It probably should have bothered me how natural it was starting to feel, drinking blood from someone's wrist. Within moments, I began to feel the disconcerting buzz beneath my skin—a sense of hot, fidgety energy overcoming me, filling me with the need to *do something*.

"Okay, come on, let's do this," I said. "Let's *move*."

But Albigard was crouching over the tub, one hand extended toward the figure lying in it. "It would be best not to jostle him more than necessary," said the Fae.

"You can sense something, I take it?" Rans asked.

Albigard nodded, not looking away from Leonides' still form. "Yes."

Zorah sounded stricken. "Uh... guys... I've been hauling him around in a fireman's carry like a sack of potatoes. We drove him here in the back of a van with horrible suspension—"

"It's not as though you could have left him where he was, love," Rans soothed. "Pull a blanket off one of the beds and we'll use it as a makeshift stretcher. We won't be moving him far."

We're moving him to freaking Chicago, I thought, a bit hysterically.

But the others were already in motion, placing a blanket on the bathroom floor and lifting Leonides onto it. My stomach flipped over when I saw the smears of red and black left behind in the tub.

Rans picked up the corners of the blanket above Leonides' shoulders, and Zorah picked up the corners by his feet.

"Don't dawdle," Albigard said, his hand describing an oval in the air. "Unless you want the human to fall over when we reach the other side."

A portal burned itself into the air between the two beds, and I immediately felt the drain of Albigard pulling power from me. Given how travel via Fae portal had affected me last time, my ability to stay upright was probably going to be in question regardless of how fast we moved. Even so, I gamely rushed through the rip in reality and staggered several steps across the unfamiliar room where I reappeared, to ensure I wouldn't be in the others' way when they came through.

Zorah and Rans followed close behind with their grim burden. By the time Albigard came through and let the portal close, I was starting to feel decidedly lightheaded again. His grip on my magical energy loosened, and I sagged in relief, breathing heavily.

"Put him on the table," Albigard ordered, not sounding nearly as wiped out as I felt... which seemed somehow unfair.

I tried to take in our surroundings. The room was large. It appeared to be a kitchen, though very little effort had been put into decorating. The cabinets lacked any sort of carving or paint — they were just plain, unfinished wood. The walls were drab, and a fine coating of dust covered everything. Cobwebs hung in the corners.

A sturdy wooden butcher-block table dominated the space, and this was where the two vampires laid the body, still resting on the stolen blanket. My eyes darted away from the bald head, fissured with oozing cracks, but not before the last of my strength left me and I sat rather abruptly on the flagstone floor.

"As I said," Albigard observed dryly.

The others spared me only quick glances to make sure I wasn't about to die or something. Albigard returned to Leonides' side and resumed whatever weird diagnostic procedure he'd been doing back in the hotel room, which seemed to involve running a hand above the vampire's body without touching it.

"Zorah," Rans said, "we're at the same house Alby brought us to when we were detained at the airport last year. I believe Silver Cross Hospital is the closest blood source. Go get us some, and you might also liberate three sets of medical scrubs while you're at it. I don't think any of your clothing is salvageable."

Zorah nodded, not arguing. I got the impression she was relieved to have something positive to do.

"I'll get food, too," she said. "Albigard, do you want anything?"

The Fae made an ambiguous gesture with his free hand, which somehow managed to convey that things like eating takeout were beneath him. I gave her my phone again, so she could pull up directions. Zorah took it and mumbled thanks in response, kissing Rans briefly but fiercely before disappearing into a swirl of fog.

Rans cut another look in my direction. "Vonnie, you should rest. There are a number of bedrooms upstairs—"

But I shook my head at him. "I'm staying."

Knowing that if I tried to stand up, it was likely to end badly, I scooted back until I could lean against the front of a cabinet.

"Very well," he said after a moment. "Albigard?"

"You were correct, bloodsucker," said the Fae. "There are still several silver projectiles embedded in his flesh. The most problematic one is pressing against his heart. Really, it's somewhat surprising that transporting him so carelessly didn't cause it to penetrate and kill him outright."

I blanched, all the blood draining from my face—leaving me feeling even fainter than before.

Rans' voice grew hard. "You will not repeat those words to Zorah. *Ever*." His pale gaze cut to me. "That goes for both of you."

Albigard shrugged. "It is already done. His soul still clings to the shell, so I see no further need to speak of it."

Rans must have read in my expression that I'd sooner cut off a limb than tell Zorah she might easily have killed her grandfather while trying to save him.

"So, if we get all of the quills out of him, he'll heal?" I asked, not really daring to believe it.

"Theoretically, yes," Rans replied.

"Or the one next to his heart will pierce the organ when we try to remove it, and he'll die," Albigard added, not very helpfully in my opinion.

"Oh," I said.

Rans pulled a dagger from a hidden sheath at his back. The blade was dark—iron, perhaps, like the one I'd seen Zorah carrying.

"Right. If you'll point me in the right direction, I may as well cut out the non-critical ones," Rans said. "When you've recovered enough to assist magically, we can address the other one."

The Fae nodded agreement, and spoke without looking at me. "Adept, are you certain you wish to be here? I've seen the bloodsucker's idea of surgery, and it hails from roughly the same historical era that he does."

Rans glared at him. "Did you just call my surgical skills *medieval*?"

"I'm staying," I repeated stubbornly. "It's not like I can see any details from down here anyway."

My decision was only partly because I still didn't think I could walk without help. Somehow, I also felt like I should be here in case Leonides died. Maybe that was stupid. It seemed unlikely he could be aware of his surroundings in his current state— thank heavens. And my sitting here wasn't likely to make a blind bit of difference to the outcome. Even so, leaving felt wrong, like I was taking the coward's way out.

The pair turned their full focus toward the figure on the table, speaking in low murmurs as Albigard directed Rans to the hidden silver projectiles. I let my eyes slip closed. While I wasn't going to leave the room, that didn't mean I was in any hurry to watch, even from my limited floor-level perspective.

It was nearly unbelievable to me that the others were acting as though Leonides might recover, with only a bit of silver removal and a hemoglobin top-off. If he did survive, would he be terribly scarred? Would he be *sane*?

I shivered, hugging myself.

Rans and Albigard worked on him for what felt like nearly an hour—though, admittedly, I wasn't in any real condition to track time accurately. The weakness from a combination of portal-travel and having magical energy yanked out of me was gradually fading, to be replaced by remnants of the jittery high from downing two hits of Zorah's blood in a single day.

I was hyperaware of my skin. Well, not just my skin. My whole body.

"That is the last one you can safely remove," Albigard said.

I opened my eyes in time to see the Fae and the vampire straighten away from their patient. Steeling myself, I braced against the cabinet and managed to get to my feet. Once I was up, I felt reasonably steady, so I took a deep breath and shot a quick glance at Leonides.

A *very* quick glance. My gaze skittered away an instant later.

"He looks the same," I said. A rather horrific mental image of Leonides walking and talking, but looking permanently as he did now flashed across my mind's eye, and I gulped convulsively against nausea.

That was shallow of me, I knew. It was also a terrible insult to people who'd been disfigured by burn injuries, and to those who loved them. Yet it still made me want to cry.

"I fear there won't be much change until we tackle that last bit of silver," Rans said. "I'm not even particularly inclined to give him blood until it's safely out—mine, or anyone else's."

"Your blood can help heal him, though?" I asked. "Like it does for humans?"

"Not in quite the same way, no," Rans said. "He'll heal with any blood, but the power in mine is more concentrated by virtue of being several centuries past its sell-by date." He must have truly taken in my expression then, because his voice softened. "Never fear, Vonnie—he *will* heal. Though the process is admittedly somewhat traumatic for everyone involved, in cases this severe… hence my desire to wait until his heart is safe before beginning it."

What about my *heart?* I wondered.

"How will you get the last piece out of him?" I asked instead, looking between them.

"Using a variation of a technique with which you yourself are familiar, adept," Albigard replied, in the tone of a teacher. "Or, rather, an expansion of said technique. I will introduce water to the wound, and guide it to form a buffer between the surface of the silver and vampire flesh. Then, I will freeze it to make a solid barrier separating the projectile safely from his heart. More water—shunted to the deepest part of the wound and frozen — will gradually push the encased silver out until it can be grasped and removed from his body."

"File under 'things that would kill a human, but not a vampire,'" Rans said, taking in my expression. "With luck, Zorah will be back at about the same time Tinkerbell here gets enough of his mojo back to do his part of the job."

Albigard shot him a dark look.

"You can take more power from me if you want it," I said quickly. "I can drink a bit of Rans' blood for a boost if I need to."

"That should not be necessary," Albigard said. "Compared to a portal, this will be but a small thing."

I nodded. "Okay. But if you need to — "

"Your offer is noted, adept," Albigard said.

Rans gave me a pointed once-over. "It will take Zorah more time to finish her errands, Vonnie, and I promise nothing of import is going to happen until she's back. No offense, but you look terrible. I'm told the utilities in the house are connected; go take a shower. You'll feel better when you're not covered with blood and concrete dust."

I chewed my lower lip, uncertain — only to make a face when the aforementioned concrete dust scraped against my teeth.

"Honestly," Rans added, "the bloodstains in particular could be a distraction we don't need when he wakes up."

That decided me. I nodded, giving in. "Okay, okay, I can take a hint. Albigard, will you show me where the bathroom is?"

The Fae indicated a direction with an elegant sweep of one hand, and I headed that way. He joined me silently, ushering me first to a closet in a bedroom bare of everything except a bed frame with a mattress, and a small table. Inside were a handful of unremarkable suits and shirts—the sort of thing a middle manager or plainclothes policeman might wear.

He handed me one of the white button-down shirts. "Here—until the demonkin returns with something more suitable," he said. "What you're wearing now is good only for burning."

Unable to help myself, I shuddered, thinking of Leonides' charred flesh. Tact hadn't magically become a Fae trait since I'd seen him last, because Albigard didn't acknowledge either the *faux pas* or my reaction to it.

"Thanks," I managed.

He showed me to a bathroom and left me to it. Like the kitchen, it was spacious but plain and unadorned... almost institutional. I rummaged around in the cabinet, unearthing some dusty towels and washcloths. A half-used bar of soap lay by the sink. The mirror was as dusty as everything else, but I could see enough of my reflection to know it wouldn't have made much difference if it were clean.

Rans was right—I had enough dust, all on my own. If it weren't for the smears and tear tracks on my face, I'd look like a ghost, or perhaps a stone statue. I turned away from the disturbing picture I presented and opened the shower stall door, reaching in to confirm that there was—in fact—running water. Preferably hot.

The pipes rattled, shooting out an uneven, rusty spray for a few seconds before it settled and ran clear. I decided that at this point, even a cold shower would be better than no shower, and let it run while I peeled off my ruined clothes. After clearing the rust from the sink's pipes as well, I gave my bra and panties a quick rinse to get the worst of the grit out, knowing there would be no replacements in the immediate future.

Fortunately, the water heater appeared to be working. I adjusted the shower until it was just shy of scalding before stepping in with the bar of soap clutched in one hand. The water ran grayish brown for long minutes before most of the grime was flushed away. I scrubbed at my skin and hair with the unscented soap, wishing for my familiar shampoo and conditioner... for my familiar apartment... for my familiar *life*.

My eyes burned. I told myself it was only because of the concrete dust.

When I was clean, I reluctantly turned off the spray and stepped out. At any other point in my life, I would have expended more emotional energy worrying about the prospect of parading around in front of a pair of hot guys wearing only damp underwear and a borrowed shirt that barely reached mid-thigh. At the moment, it didn't even make the list of things to fret over.

I used the damp towel to wipe most of the dust off my shoes and put them on, sans socks. My hair was a tangled disaster, but I didn't even have a hair tie to pull it back, much less a comb. For lack of any other options, I let it curl wildly around my face.

It wasn't too difficult to retrace my steps to the kitchen. When I reached it, Zorah was there. She thrust a square of folded blue fabric and a greasy paper bag that smelled of fast food at me.

"Eat," she said, before thrusting a less greasy bag at Albigard. "You, too."

Albigard took the offering with a put-upon sigh and retrieved a salad in a plastic container from its depths. I set the food aside on a handy counter, just long enough to toe off my shoes and pull on the thin cotton scrub pants. They were a couple of inches too long, but I ignored the poor fit. Shoes back on, I attacked the food, carefully not looking in the direction of the butcher-block table in the center of the room as I ate.

He'll be okay soon, I told myself firmly. *Zorah's back with the blood. They can heal him now.*

I finished the burger and fries way too fast, shoveling the food down like a ravenous hyena. Albigard was still picking at his salad, but he met my eyes when I turned to him.

"Are you ready?" I asked. "Can we do it now?"

The Fae set the plastic fork aside. "Yes, adept. Let us see if we can fix your nightcrawler without breaking his heart."

ELEVEN

"Very well," Rans agreed. "Zorah, get the blood bags ready for him. I'll let him tap me first, to jump-start his healing."

Zorah shot me a worried look. "Should Vonnie wait somewhere else while we do this?" Her expression turned apologetic. "Nothing personal, babe—it's just that you have a heartbeat."

"So does Albigard," I pointed out, ignoring the little shiver of instinctive disquiet her words brought about. "And shouldn't I be close by, in case he ends up needing to pull power from me after all?"

"I won't," Albigard said flatly.

Rans gave me an assessing look. "I can control Guthrie; I'm his sire… not to mention, a good deal older and more powerful. But you've never seen a vampire overcome by bloodlust, Vonnie. It's not a pretty sight. It's also not a side of him that he would likely want you to see."

A chill swept through me. Was I ready to see a man—one who prided himself on his control—have that control stripped from him? *Bloodlust*, Rans called it. The term was evocative, bringing to mind every half-remembered vampire horror movie I'd ever seen.

But could I call myself Leonides' friend if I shied from seeing that side of him? More importantly, what if Albigard *did* end up needing help, and I was hiding away at the far end of the enormous house? I would never be able to forgive myself.

"I'll stay," I said. "God knows he's already seen *me* at my worst."

And he'd never run away—not once. He'd never offered anything more pointed than the occasional dry, teasing quip about the state of my dumpster fire of a life. Unbidden, I remembered the cool solace of his aura as he sheltered me through Dhuinne's dark night, while madness howled all around me, nipping at my heels.

Rans' gaze pinned mine for a moment more before he nodded his agreement.

"Stand over there," he said, indicating the corner by the door. "Try not to be alarmed by anything you see. As I'm sure you've gathered, he won't be himself at first." He paused. "Oh... and despite what it will look like, he won't be doing me any permanent damage."

Zorah's expression was grim. "Though you might want to lose the shirt first, lover. He'll do some permanent damage to *that*, and I'm kind of fond of it."

Rans looked down at the cream-colored poet shirt he was wearing beneath a black vest. "Good point. Pardon the unintended exhibitionism, you lot."

"I'm not complaining," Zorah said, as he stripped off the clothing and tossed it onto a nearby counter—though her heart didn't seem to be in it.

For my part, I would never have considered going into sex work if I'd been bothered by the sight of male nipples in the general course of things. But with Zorah's succubus blood still buzzing around my system, I had to look away from his bare, toned torso quickly to keep from flushing.

My eyes fell on Leonides instead. The sight of his burned body instantly quashed any other thoughts or physical reactions. Now that we were finally poised to do something about it, I could no longer avoid the reality of the damage that had been done to him. I was vaguely aware of Zorah dropping an insulated carry-bag next to the table and pulling a couple of blood bags out of it.

Albigard crossed to the kitchen sink and pulled a dusty mug out of one of the cabinets. He rinsed it and filled it with water... and suddenly, it was time to enact this crazy plan. I rolled my lower lip between my teeth—a nervous gesture—still barely able to comprehend the idea of the sad figure with its missing skin and cracked, weeping flesh being anything other than dead.

His soul still clings to the shell, Albigard had said. Now we just had to make sure it stayed that way while the Fae pulled a razor-sharp silver shard away from Leonides' heart.

Albigard set the mug of tap water down on the table near Leonides' head. He gestured to Rans, and the vampire handed him the dagger he'd used earlier to cut out the rest of the silver. Albigard took the iron blade gingerly, and opened a slice in the space between Leonides' ribs, like someone butchering a side of meat. My stomach roiled. Zorah's mouth pressed into a thin, bloodless line.

I had a clear view of the proceedings as Albigard set aside the blade and lifted the mug with one hand. He tipped a thin stream of water over the wound, the fingers of his other hand somehow directing the flow without touching it. When he was satisfied, he set the mug aside again, lifting both hands to hover palm-down over Leonides' chest. His green eyes slipped closed in concentration.

My pendant throbbed as magic swirled around the table. Distantly, I wondered if Fae adepts controlled water the same way I did, by channeling their emotions. Not that I'd seen much evidence of emotion from Albigard in our brief acquaintance— at least, not much beyond disdain and vague irritation.

The form on the table shuddered, and I caught my breath.

"Hold him," Albigard said.

Rans, standing by Leonides' head, placed a hand on each burned shoulder, pressing him down as his torso jerked. I covered my mouth with one hand, the heady confirmation that Leonides was truly alive competing with the sickening knowledge that he must be regaining awareness, as the water buffered the silver spike inside him, separating it from his flesh.

He had to be in the worst kind of agony imaginable.

Albigard poured more water into the wound and waved a hand over it. Leonides bucked hard against Rans' hold. The Fae splayed one hand over the scorched flesh of Leonides' ribcage to help restrain him, and fished around in the gash he'd sliced open with the other. A moment later, he came up with a blood-tinged shard of ice—something metallic glinting at its center.

Leonides arched and screamed.

"Stand back," Rans snapped at the Fae, pitching his voice to be heard over the sounds of utter torment. "Zorah, be ready with the blood bags."

Albigard melted backward, coming to a stop by the sink. He tossed the frozen silver projectile into it with a sharp clink.

Rans continued to pin Leonides in place as the injured man writhed, his cries rising and falling in pitch like a wounded animal's. Trapped air burned inside my chest, but I didn't dare breathe for fear of what kind of sounds might come out of my mouth. I couldn't watch, but I couldn't look away. Tears blurred my vision.

When I blinked past the curtain of wetness, it was to see the impossible happening. New skin crept across the terrible patchwork of exposed muscle and sinew—crawling over clotted blood and weeping, blistered flesh. The breath burst from my lungs in a soft cry. I stared at the miraculously healing body, feeling dizzy and lightheaded.

It must have been torture. I could remember all too well the way it felt when serious injuries knitted themselves back together impossibly fast under the influence of vampire blood. But my bullet wounds and broken bones had been *nothing* compared to this.

For long minutes, we watched helplessly as Leonides' body put itself back together, inch by tortuous inch. Bits of burned clothing that had melted into flesh sloughed off as the skin reformed beneath them. He flopped around on the table, trying to rise with uncoordinated movements. Gradually, I became aware of a low, soothing counterpoint to his anguished cries—Rans murmuring words of comfort, telling him it would be over soon and he could have blood… telling him to hold on a little bit longer.

My throat tightened. Leonides hadn't wanted this life… this *undeath*. He'd wanted Rans to let him go, so he could finally escape from his century-long existence bound to a demon. But now, not even this terrible injury could kill him… and I felt like I should somehow be angry on his behalf. Yet all I could feel was relief.

Selfish, thoughtless relief.

The figure was becoming recognizably human now—naked and hairless, and far too gaunt, as though his body was consuming itself to rebuild all the parts that had been broken. His hands clutched at the edges of the table like claws, wood cracking and splintering under the force of his grip. His hoarse cries morphed into growls of rage.

Bloodlust.

"Right," Rans said. "That's good enough to be getting on with. Up you come, mate. Get some of this into you."

Leonides' eyes snapped open and immediately locked on me, lit from within with a terrible glow. He looked feral, his face twisted into a rictus of animal need. Rans stepped around to stand at his side, blocking his view of me, one hand still locked firmly on his shoulder.

"No. Not the one with the heartbeat. That's not what you need," he said firmly. "Come here."

Leonides lunged upright, slamming into Rans and burying his teeth in the other vampire's neck so fast that the movement looked like a blur to my human eyes. The attack sent Rans staggering back a step before he braced himself against the onslaught. I, on the other hand, stumbled backward until my shoulders thumped against the wall, blank shock thrumming through me.

I'd known, intellectually, what to expect.

Somehow, that didn't help.

Dark blood trickled down Rans' back from the juncture of his neck and shoulder, where Leonides was tearing into the grisly bite wound like a terrier with a rat. Rather than fighting back, though, the older vampire held Leonides' head in place with a hand wrapped around the nape of his neck.

I watched, frozen in place, as dark hair sprouted across Leonides' scalp. Rans let him rip and tear and suck for longer than I would've thought he could tolerate it. Finally, though, he said a few low words and tightened his grip on Leonides' nape, plucking him away from his grisly meal.

Leonides snarled and spat, and I would hardly have credited Rans' power over him if I hadn't felt a fresh throb of magic in the room. *I can control Guthrie; I'm his sire*, Rans had said, as though the simple statement was an unbreakable maxim. Rans had created Leonides. Apparently, that meant Rans could master his feral nature even under these extreme circumstances.

Already, the torn flesh at the side of Rans' neck was closing over, only the streaks of drying blood trailing down his back remaining as evidence of the feeding frenzy. Leonides' violet-lit gaze roamed the room, once again fixing firmly on me. Suddenly, my heartbeat in my ears sounded unbearably loud.

"No," Rans said again. "Not her. Zorah?"

Zorah hurried forward with one of the blood bags held out in front of her. Leonides snarled again and tore it from her grip almost too quickly for me to follow, ripping into it with his teeth. It seemed worse, seeing him act like this, now that he once again looked almost like his old self. I stood with my back pressed flat against the wall, paralyzed like a rabbit faced with a ravenous wolf. As Zorah proffered another bag of blood to replace the one now drained and shredded, I consciously unclenched my muscles one by one.

This was what the others had tried to warn me about. But my reply at the time still held. Leonides was a vampire. He hadn't chosen to be, but he was one nevertheless. If I claimed to care about him, that meant I cared about his vampire side as much as his human side. This insatiable beast—the vampire with blood running in rivulets down his chin to splatter against his broad chest—was the reason Leonides had been able to mesmerize Ivan to forget about the debt Richard and I owed him. It was the reason he'd been able to shelter me on Dhuinne... the reason his blood could heal me and strengthen my magic.

If Leonides hadn't been a vampire, he couldn't have saved Zorah by turning her when she nearly died while escaping the Fae. He couldn't have overpowered half a dozen SWAT officers when we'd been trapped in the woods together. Also, the never-ending vampire jokes at the Vixen's Den wouldn't have been half as funny.

This.

Was.

Leonides.

Not all of him, certainly. Not an aspect he would want me to see, I was sure. But this was also a part of his truth. This was the darker side of what Rans had made him.

I took a hesitant step away from the wall. Across the room, Albigard stood against the sink, arms crossed, a look of mild distaste on his finely shaped features. Blood bag followed blood bag, until Zorah had no more to give him. Leonides dropped to his knees and buried his face in his hands, his spine bowed beneath the weight of the day. Rans crouched in front of him, sitting on his heels — watching him intently, but remaining silent.

Leonides' shoulders shook. I took another step toward him, drawn to that pained tremor like a moth to flame. His head shot up, his violet gaze meeting Rans' and then Zorah's, dark with alarm.

"Vonnie!" he said sharply. "The building... did she — "

"I'm right here," I said, my voice unsteady. "I'm okay... Zorah saved both of us."

The fear in his voice made something ache, deep in my chest. At the same time, the realization that he'd fixated on my heartbeat in his desperation for blood, and hadn't known it was *me*, stirred a frisson of disquiet.

That disquiet fled beneath the look of absolute relief in his expression when he craned around to see me, following the sound of my voice. My eyes slid down to the blood drying on his lips and jaw — I couldn't help myself. An instant later he turned his face away, hiding it from me.

"Yeah, don't listen to a word of what she's saying," Zorah said, seemingly heedless of the awkward moment. "I didn't save her. She saved herself. I just showed her which part of the wall to blow out with a blast of magic. Then she masterminded a van theft to get the three of us away from there, and helped Tinkerbell portal us here to his creepy warded house in Chicago."

Leonides gave a small nod, acknowledging her words, but didn't look up. Rans sighed and rose to his feet.

"Right. Come on, old friend. Let's find you a hot shower and a bar of soap. We'll tackle the rest of it in the morning."

He reached down and hooked Leonides by the upper arm, hauling him to his feet. Leonides rose with the pull, weaving unsteadily until Rans and Zorah steadied him from either side. They turned and led him toward the door... a long, dark shape between them, either unaware or uncaring of his own nakedness. I remained frozen in place, two steps from the wall as they passed me to leave the room. Leonides kept his face averted, shame radiating from the hunched curve of his shoulders.

And then they were gone.

TWELVE

Albigard hadn't moved from his position propping up the kitchen counter, his arms folded across his chest. He remained silent as the sound of shuffling footsteps faded, but I could feel his eyes on me. I bore it for several seconds, until I abruptly couldn't anymore.

"What?" I snapped.

He raised a slow eyebrow.

"Goddamn it," I said. "If you've got something to say, just say it."

The eyebrow lowered. "If you insist."

I waited for a beat.

"*Well*?"

The Fae sighed. "Merely this. As distasteful as the prospect sounds—if you insist on pursuing this course, you'd do well to ask one of them to turn you sooner rather than later."

I blinked, trying to sort through that rather cryptic statement. "Uh… pursuing *what* course? Please don't talk in riddles, Albigard. I don't really have the brainpower to spare right now."

Albigard managed to convey the sense of an eye-roll without breaking expression. I wondered if Leonides had learned that skill from him, or vice versa.

"You're in love with him, for some incomprehensible reason," said the Fae. "But, as you have just seen, he will live until he manages to get himself staked or decapitated... or until his demon succeeds in extracting itself from its current predicament and decides to take revenge on him. You, on the other hand, are a mayfly. One shock to the heart or snap of a vertebra, and you'll be gone, like rain soaked up by the earth."

I stared at him. "What the *hell* are you talking about? I don't... I'm not..."

He made a short, scoffing noise. "Not to mention the fact that allowing yourself to be turned would free you of much of the burden of your soul-debt to me—in practice, if not in theory. I assure you, I would have to be quite desperate indeed to resort to pulling magic from a vampire. Pulling human magic is bad enough."

Silence stretched for a long moment.

"You know, Leonides was right," I managed. "You really are kind of an asshole."

An amused glint flashed in his green eyes, but I didn't stick around to continue trading verbal salvoes with him. Instead, I cast around until I saw Rans' shirt and the scrubs Zorah had stolen, sitting in a messy pile on the counter. Scooping everything up, I exited stage left, trying not to let his words take root as I retraced the path to the bathroom he had showed me earlier.

It was empty. Since I was already committed—and since the others really *would* need the clothing—I began a quick search of the sprawling house. It was two stories tall, with steps leading down to an unfinished basement. The place appeared to be built on a symmetrical floor plan, with four bedrooms, four baths, and large common rooms on both levels.

Honestly, it was a bit surprising this house hadn't been snapped up by developers and subdivided into cheap apartments before now... or maybe that's what the wards were for. Maybe no one could even tell the house was here unless they'd been given permission to enter, or already knew to look for it.

Thanks to Murphy's Law, I ended up finding the three vampires in the last bathroom I checked. The hard pattering sound of a running shower drew me to the door, which was open. I knocked awkwardly on the doorframe rather than barging in. Zorah glanced over from her perch on the closed lid of the toilet and hopped up to meet me. Rans was leaning against the vanity; his gaze remained fixed on the oversized shower stall.

"I brought clothes," I told Zorah, proffering the sad collection.

She took the pile from me and set it next to the sink. "Thanks, hon. I forgot all about that."

Rans caught the shirt she tossed at him and wordlessly shrugged into it. Zorah started stripping off her burned garments and replacing them with scrubs, apparently not bothered by my presence. I glanced away, still uncomfortably aware of the way the blood I'd drunk from her heated my skin, skittering along my nerves like champagne bubbles whenever my eyes were drawn to bare flesh.

It was safer to let my attention wander around the bathroom. This was one of two larger bathrooms on the upper story... not that the one I'd used downstairs had been small, by any means. But here, in addition to the vanity, toilet, and shower stall—this one easily big enough for two people—there was also an extravagant garden-style tub in the corner, and two sinks rather than one.

Helpless to avoid it, my eyes were drawn to the shower door. Steam and frosted glass obscured the details within, but I could make out the dark shape of Leonides hunched in a ball on the floor as the water streamed over him.

Is he all right? I wanted to ask. But I swallowed the words, knowing Leonides would be able to hear them, and wouldn't appreciate them. Of course he wasn't *all right*—he'd been burnt to a crisp while still alive, and then had descended into a ravenous blood-craze during his recovery.

"Are you two okay?" I asked instead. "It's been... kind of a day."

Rans had cleaned the drying gore off his neck and back, and Zorah had already shed her coating of dust and grime from the collapsed building—apparently by virtue of transforming into mist and back.

"Yeah, no permanent harm done," Zorah assured me. "Told you, vampires are tough."

"You're not kidding," I muttered, Albigard's words circling like restless vultures above my thoughts. Once again, I set them firmly aside to think about later.

Or, y'know, *not*.

A vaguely uncomfortable silence settled over the room, broken only by the splatter of water drops against glass. I hovered by the door, not entirely sure I was welcome in this intimate setting, but unwilling to leave. I needed to see Leonides back to his old self. I needed to know we'd really saved him.

After an age, the crouched form in the shower uncurled, rising to its feet. The water slowed to a trickle, then a drip. Leonides paused and stood unmoving for several moments, before he finally stretched out a hand and opened the sliding door.

I couldn't have stopped my eyes drinking in his unmarked body any more than I could stop my own heart from beating. He was... as he had always been, with one exception. His hair had grown back, perhaps to the same length it had been the night he'd been turned into a vampire. At least, a similar thing had happened to Zorah after the fire had scorched her wild curls—they'd grown back, but her roots were now uneven where the coloring had grown out.

I was used to seeing Leonides with short, thick dreads. Now, his naturally kinky hair flopped across his forehead, dripping wet. He palmed it out of his face. As though he'd just registered my presence, he went suddenly still. I heard a sharp, indrawn breath before he gave a slight shudder and dragged his attention away from me, to Rans.

"Jesus," he said hoarsely. "I'm still hungry. How the hell can I still be hungry?"

His hand gripped the edge of the shower door hard enough that I feared for the integrity of the metal frame. Rans gave a one-shouldered shrug, studiously casual.

"Try not to worry about it, mate. Like Vonnie said, it's been rather a day."

Zorah, looking out of place in her borrowed scrubs, crossed her arms and tapped her fingers on her forearm. "I could go to another hospital. Pick you up a few more pints. It wouldn't take long, and one of us will need to venture out soon to get some essentials anyway."

"You can have my blood," I blurted, not having planned the words ahead of time in any way, shape, or form. I swallowed, letting my brain catch up before continuing a bit sheepishly, "I mean—by this point, half of it's probably yours anyhow."

His eyes flared amethyst, before he screwed them shut for a moment, obviously reaching for control. When he opened them, natural brown dominated again, only a pinprick of light remaining. "Vonnie, I—"

"No, I'm serious," I said, hurrying to cut him off. "It's fine. Rans can… make sure you don't get carried away. If that's still an issue, I mean," I hurried to add. "Right, Rans?"

Rans had been watching the exchange with a complicated expression on his handsome features. At that, his eyes flicked to Zorah's for an instant. I almost missed the tiny nod she gave in response, but then he nodded as well, his face settling into neutral lines.

"Very well. I suppose that's the most straightforward method of dealing with the issue for now. Are you in control of yourself?"

I turned to Leonides in time to see his throat bob as he swallowed.

"Well… yes, but—"

"No 'buts,'" I told him, barreling headfirst down this road before anyone could tell me I was holding the map upside down.

I undid the top few buttons of Albigard's borrowed shirt and pulled the collar aside, baring my neck and collarbone. And there it was again—that faint intake of breath, from a vampire who didn't need to breathe. His eyes zeroed in on my jugular like iron filings pulled by a magnet. Something jumped low in my belly—warm, insistent, and desperately inappropriate for the situation.

Damned succubus blood.

But apparently, recklessness had become my thing now. When the hell had that happened? My heart fluttered… fear, combined with something hotter. Fortunately, I caught myself in time to reinforce the focus inside my pendant, before anything *outside* the barrier of my skin started smoldering.

A folded towel smacked into Leonides' broad chest. He fumbled it, finally tearing his eyes away from my neck to frown at Zorah.

She looked heavenward. "Do us a favor and cover your bare ass first, yeah? I might be part sex demon, but this is still weirding me out, *Grandpa*."

A faint snort, barely audible, came from Rans' direction, and I felt my face heat. Leonides continued to glare at both of them, but he did wrap the towel around his waist. When his attention landed on me again, it occurred to me exactly what I was doing—I could have rolled up a sleeve and stuck my wrist out for him. But no, instead I'd unbuttoned my freaking shirt and yanked it down, baring more boobage to the room than even my sluttiest 'escort' dress would have shown.

And now it was too late to back out. Not... that I *wanted* to back out, exactly. I just wasn't sure I needed Zorah and Rans in here watching us.

But, of course, there was the small matter of also not wanting Leonides to accidentally drain me to death in a momentary loss of control. I'd seen what he'd done to Rans, not half an hour ago. In fact, what I was offering to do now was probably crazy, given that very fact.

But Leonides was already in front of me, looking down with twin violet pinpricks of light kindling in his dark eyes, his brows forming a little furrow between them. I could feel the humidity coming off his dark skin... see the tiny drops of water beading on his face and chest.

He didn't make it worse by refusing what I'd offered and insisting on a wrist after all. He *did* lift a hand, one finger tracing down the side of my throat until it caught on the chain of my necklace, which would presumably still be invisible to him. My head rolled to the side in response to the light touch, completely without conscious volition. I felt the tiny gold links slide out of the way, and then his head was bending down. My eyes slipped closed as cool lips brushed against sensitive skin.

"I'm sorry, Vonnie," he murmured.

The low vibration of his voice sent goosebumps down my arms, but I only had an instant to wonder what he was apologizing for before two sharp points slid into my tender flesh. I gasped. A large hand cradled the back of my head, holding me in place to prevent me instinctively trying to jerk away, doing more damage to myself in the process.

Leonides' fingers tangled in my hair at the same time I felt a deep pull at my neck, sending a confusing jangle of conflicting signals along my nerves. My knees wobbled, and I locked them.

The pain was still there, sort of. And I did feel decidedly dizzy. But there was something else — a slow tide of heat. A sort of connection, like there was more than just my blood flowing between us.

My blood. Jesus Christ, I was letting a *vampire* drink my *blood.* And it wasn't nearly as terrifying as it should have been, because recently I'd been drinking *his* blood — and Zorah's, and Rans' — like it was absinthe and I was Vincent van Gogh on a month-long bender.

Also, that realization wasn't doing a damned thing to cool the heat rushing through me. I was suddenly quite relieved that I'd taken time to wash my bra in the sink earlier, otherwise the whole room would have a view of my nipples trying to drill holes through Albigard's white silk-blend shirt.

The bra might've been all right, but I had a terrible feeling my panties were ruined again.

Before my dizziness had a chance to progress beyond 'pleasantly floaty' to 'dancing gray spots in my vision,' I felt the deeply unpleasant sensation of Leonides' fangs sliding free of my neck. I was aware of blood pulsing from the open wounds, caught within the seal of the soft lips still pressed to my skin. A tongue rasped across the raw holes, simultaneously stinging and deeply, unavoidably arousing. I fumbled mentally to make sure I wasn't letting any magic leak past my control.

The sting faded, replaced by a faint tingle, and Leonides straightened away, his hand sliding free of my hair in favor of cupping my shoulder to ensure I was steady on my feet. While 'steady' might have been overstating things a bit, I wasn't drained to the point of being debilitated. He'd maintained control. He hadn't hurt me. I'd offered blood, and he'd taken only enough to blunt the edge of his hunger.

I lifted a hand to where the wounds should have been. There was nothing — just smooth skin.

"It's already healed," he said quietly.

"So it is," I agreed. I knew well enough that vampire blood healed wounds. Apparently vampire saliva did as well. "Are you... um... are you feeling better?"

It was an idiotic thing to ask, really. One look at Leonides' face was enough to tell me he wasn't.

He hesitated for a moment before replying. "Less hungry, anyway." Another pause. "Thank you."

I shrugged and tried to play it off. "Oh, it was nothing. Like I said, half of it was yours to start with, right? It only seems fair."

And... now I was babbling. I snapped my mouth shut before more words could come tumbling out.

Rans straightened from his spot leaning against the edge of the vanity. "So. Next steps," he said in a brisk tone. "Rest, obviously. And Zorah's right that we'll need to make a run for supplies. I'll do that, since everyone else here has either been impaled by sentient thorns or had a building fall on them recently."

I thought I saw Leonides wince, though he covered it quickly. Had the others filled him in on what, exactly, had happened after the gas leak exploded?

"Sounds like a plan," Zorah said. "Let's see. Someone needs to let Len know we're okay. We also need more blood. Food for a few days. Clothing that isn't scrubs. Toiletries. Vonnie, what size are you? An eight? Thirty-six-D bra size?"

One good thing about having your blood drained was that it was easier to keep from blushing afterward. "Thirty-six-C." I cleared my throat, thinking of Leonides' regrown hair flopping over his forehead and hoping I wasn't about to significantly overstep my bounds. "Can I add a couple other things to get?"

"Certainly," Rans said. "In fact, why don't you and Zorah go make a proper list? See what Tinkerbell needs while you're at it. I'll get Guthrie settled in a room, and be on my way while the stores are still open. I'll find a discreet way to contact Len while I'm out."

It was telling—not to mention worrying—that Leonides didn't immediately jump in with some testy remark about not needing a pasty English twat to act as a babysitter. Indeed, the lack of any sort of irritable retort hung in the air awkwardly. Zorah cast him a worried look, but she led me out of the steamy bathroom rather than say anything directly.

"What else did you need?" she asked, as we headed back downstairs in search of Albigard.

"A size-six crochet hook and some shea butter." *And possibly, my head examined.*

She looked confused for a moment, then surprised. Her features smoothed out. "Good thought," she said. "Not sure he'll sit still for it, but... well, you already know that."

"Is he going to be okay, though?" I blurted, unable to help myself this time.

There was a thoughtful silence before she replied. "We made a mistake in judgment, and I'm guessing people died," she said eventually. "Not all of the tenants were out of the building when the place went up. That's going to eat at him—you know how he gets sometimes. There's also the part where he hates the fact that Rans and I made him a vampire, and he doesn't like to be reminded of the dark side of being undead."

I supposed that descending into uncontrolled bloodlust would be... a pretty big reminder. But...

"I'm just glad he survived," I whispered.

A slender hand wrapped around my shoulder, and Zorah pulled me against her side in a brief, one-armed hug as we walked.

"I know how you feel," she said.

THIRTEEN

Rans left to shop for a few days' supplies for us. The logical thing for me to do at that point would have been to get some sleep. He and Zorah had already claimed one of the downstairs bedrooms, and Albigard, the other.

That left the two larger upstairs suites. Leonides had taken the one attached to the bathroom where he'd showered earlier, so I took the remaining bedroom. It was devoid of anything beyond an unmade bed, a small table, a chair, and an empty closet—but the boiler in the basement was running, and the steam radiator next to the wall had warmed the room to a pleasant temperature.

I lay on the bare mattress in my borrowed shirt. I'd left the overhead light turned on, and was staring at the ceiling with unfocused eyes, unable to sleep. And really, sleep would have been *super-useful*, because at this point I was utterly exhausted. Mild blood loss... adrenaline crash... surviving a building collapse... whichever way you looked at it, my body was completely justified in its need for rest.

Unfortunately, my nerves didn't appear to see it that way. Hours later, and my double dose of succubus blood was still tingling away beneath my skin. Add to that, the endlessly circling litany of worries that more or less defined my life these days. Jace. Richard. Teague. The other missing children. My apparent destruction of my friendship with Len. Albigard's troubling words about becoming a vampire, which I still refused to think about. The small matter of the world maybe ending soon if we couldn't do something to stop it.

And now, Leonides. In my mind, my ex-boss was some larger-than-life figure. Untouchable— though after Dhuinne, there was a certain irony attached to the use of that adjective. *Indomitable*, then… with emotional walls thicker than Fort Knox.

But he sure hadn't looked very 'indomitable' when I'd left him alone in the bathroom with Rans, wrapped in a threadbare towel and refusing to meet anyone's gaze.

God.

I pressed the heels of my hands against my eye sockets. Somehow, the idea of Leonides *not being all right* was scarier than half of the other vaguely apocalyptic things on my worry list. I needed him to be all right. Because—and this was the truly terrifying part—I wasn't at all sure I could do this without him.

There was a faint rustle outside my door, followed by the sound of light footsteps moving away. For lack of anything better to do, I rolled to my feet and padded across the room. The door hinges creaked, light spilling into the hallway to reveal a pile of bags outside the room, containing clothing and other necessities. A note, scrawled in a messy hand, poked out of the topmost bag.

Do you have any idea how difficult it is to find a crochet needle? In Chicago? AT THIS HOUR??

Any other time, I might've appreciated the attempt at humor. As it was, I dragged the bags into my borrowed room and sorted everything out, removing tags as I went. There was, indeed, a crochet hook and a plastic tub of shea butter included.

The mindless organizing should have soothed me. It didn't. But at least I had clean underwear now.

I blinked at the empty bed, dreading the idea of climbing back into it to stare blankly at the ceiling some more. What time was it? I had no clue, since I'd neglected to get my phone back from Zorah after lending it to her earlier. Maybe I was happier not knowing.

A growing compulsion to check on Leonides made my feet feel restless. And... under the circumstances, surely that wasn't an irrational urge. He'd nearly died. I'd nearly died. The idea of looking in on him to make sure he was all right seemed rational enough. Just a quick check to see if he needed anything, and maybe to float the idea that had occurred to me earlier.

I took a deep breath and ventured into the hall, leaving the bedroom light on behind me. That, combined with moonlight filtering in from the windows, was enough to keep me from running into anything—not that there was much here to run into. The central space on the top floor was meant to be a living room, but it was empty of furniture. The large staircase leading to the main floor was a dark pit. Beyond the landing lay an empty room that might've been an office or study. Then the large bathroom, and finally, the bedroom.

Unlike me, Leonides had left his pile of bags and packages untouched in the hall. I knocked, softly enough that it hopefully wouldn't wake a sleeper, even if that sleeper was a vampire.

Silence reigned for a beat.

"Get some sleep, Vonnie."

The words filtered to me through the closed door.

"Can't sleep," I shot back, keeping my voice low because he'd be able to hear me regardless. "I'm coming in."

I turned the knob and entered, figuring we were past the point of standing on ceremony. He'd seen me naked and coming around his fingers; I'd seen him naked and tearing at the flesh of someone's throat. Compared to that, finding him lying on his back in the dark, wearing only a pair of scrub bottoms was fairly anticlimactic. I came to a stop just inside the room, and he rolled into a sitting position on the edge of the bed, watching me in the pale moonlight.

I cleared my throat. "Hey… so, I asked Rans to pick up some stuff I could use to —"

He cut me off, something I couldn't ever remember him doing before.

"You drank Zorah's blood," he said, a hint of tightness in his voice. "It must've been you, right? Rans didn't have a reason to drink from her — not when she was hurt and he wasn't."

I blinked at him. "Um… yes. I did. Twice. My arm was crushed under the rubble. And afterward,

I needed to boost my magic so Albigard could draw from me to get us here through a portal." I swallowed and licked my lips. "So, the others. Did they already tell you what happened? To the building, I mean."

He looked away. "Yeah. I know it's gone. I know about the Fae shrapnel bomb made of silver spikes. And that you and Zorah got me out of there somehow."

It was my turn to look away. "Well... *she* did. I mostly hid behind some trashcans in an alley."

"And stole a van," he added. "And got us away from St. Louis."

"Borrowed," I muttered. "I *borrowed* a van. And that was still thanks to Zorah's mesmerism, more than anything."

More silence.

He shifted on the bed. "The death toll. What was it?"

I took a deep breath, forcing it past the growing tightness in my throat. "I don't know. There's no TV in this place that I've seen, and Zorah has my phone. Rans might have checked the news while he was out."

"Not all the tenants had gone," Leonides said, the words barely audible. "I didn't bother to make them leave. I... didn't take the time."

My chest ached. "Part of the building sheared off. But the rest of it was still standing when we left. Emergency services were there with rescue equipment. They might have been okay."

"Or they could've been killed." A faint, choked noise stuck in his throat. "You could've been killed.

You were buried in rubble. Vonnie... *you could have died.*"

I thought you were dead, too. My breath caught on the words. It was all I could do to keep them from escaping into the empty space between us. The broken noise as my chest shuddered against a sob made it past my control, however—and I couldn't have stopped my feet crossing the distance separating us if my life depended on it.

The next thing I knew, I was half-straddling his lap with my arms wrapped around him—one knee braced on the edge of the mattress, and the other foot still on the floor. Honestly, I expected him to freeze beneath the embrace, or maybe push me away. I did *not* expect callused hands to bury themselves in my hair, dragging my mouth to his.

I could feel his full lips on mine... his tongue demanding entrance. Fangs scraped against my lips and I tasted blood, the tiny wounds healing almost as fast as they appeared beneath the power of his saliva. A moan wrenched its way free from one of us—me, I was pretty sure. Somehow I was fully in his lap now, and fire was spreading through my veins, as the kiss grew more frantic.

Everything that had been seething beneath my skin since St. Louis came bursting free like lava overflowing a volcano. I felt hands roaming my back possessively, and cool skin under my own clutching fingers. Abruptly, the acrid scent of something far less metaphorical beginning to smolder reached me. I pulled back with a gasp, frantically reorienting my magic before it could take hold and catch something on fire.

Leonides made a sound like a growl, his hands closing around the meat of my thighs. My balance shifted abruptly as he rose, lifting me with him as though my weight meant nothing to him. I wrapped arms and legs around him, clinging. My head fell back as his mouth fell on the same spot on my neck where his fangs had pierced earlier.

Dizzy with need, all I could do was hang on as he carried me effortlessly through a second door in the room that had apparently been standing open. The space beyond was darker... windowless. Some sense of fleeting familiarity told me it must be the en suite bathroom where he'd drunk my blood beneath Rans and Zorah's watchful gaze.

My ass hit something hard and cold with a sharp edge — the vanity. My legs were still wrapped around his waist, but he pulled away far enough that he could grasp the edges of Albigard's shirt and tug. Buttons popped free of their holes, some of them flying off to ping against tile and glass. I took advantage of the gap between us to tug at the drawstring waist of his loose pants, needing skin on skin even if it meant having to let go with my legs for a minute.

It was awkward and clumsy, and might have been less so if I could only see a damned thing in the dark. But *he* could see. Eventually we managed to get each other naked. I thanked my lucky stars for his foresight when he picked me up again and carried me into the ridiculously large shower stall, because I seriously doubted my ability to focus well enough to keep from setting my surroundings aflame.

Water hissed through the pipes, a few cold drops spattering me past the shelter of Leonides' body before it warmed. *Blood warm*, I thought in a daze, feeling the pulse of urgency through my veins and arteries as our bodies pressed together.

He set my back against the wall, my body under the spray — sharp drops stinging my skin and waking every thrumming nerve. An ankle between mine shoved my feet apart, widening my stance. I slapped a palm behind me to steady myself, my senses spinning. Leonides dropped to his knees in front of me in the dark. Large hands grasped my hips, thumbs pressing into the creases of my thighs an instant before his mouth closed over my sex.

I let out a thoroughly embarrassing high-pitched squeak of shock, which dissolved into a choked cry when his tongue rasped along the length of my slit. He dove into me like a starving man, tongue curling and delving. My hand that wasn't splayed against the shower wall for balance somehow ended up tangled in his messy spirals of hair, clutching helplessly. The hard tug wrenched a groan from him, the sound of it vibrating directly against my overheated flesh.

God — it seemed impossible that this feeling had been foreign to me mere days ago. Already, I could feel the sense of something tightening deep inside me… winding up like a spring. His thumbs slid closer to my center, pressing in and spreading my outer lips to further bare me to his mouth.

The tongue that had been fucking into me flattened and dragged deliciously over my clit. I shuddered hard, water entering my mouth as my lips parted in a gasp. Drops spattered sharply against my breasts, stinging against the painfully erect points of my nipples. Leonides' tongue slid over and over my sensitive nub, the flat of it dragging across nerves stretched tight.

One of his hands left its place cupping my hipbone—all the warning I had before two fingers plunged inside me, moving in time with the wet slide of his tongue across my clit. I wailed as an orgasm crashed through me. My second one ever, and if anything, it was more powerful than the one he'd gifted me in Dhuinne.

Leonides didn't let up until my wail rose to a shriek and my knees started to give out. Then, he was there, holding me up, his cheek pressed against my stomach. Past the thundering echo of my own heartbeat, I could feel faint shivers going through his body.

As I gradually started to come back to myself, I gentled the hand that had been fisting his hair hard enough that it surely must have hurt.

"Leo," I breathed, still blind in the dark with the water streaming over me.

He rose, his wet body sliding against mine on the way up, until I was once more supported by his hands cupping my ass. My arms and legs wrapped around him instinctively, and this time, I could feel the hard press of his erection against me.

"God, *yes*," I whispered, and felt his breath stutter out in a harsh exhalation.

I wriggled, needing that hardness an inch or so to the left in the same way as I needed my next breath. The sensation as he lined himself up and let gravity slide me down onto that thick length was like nothing I'd ever experienced. I could feel him in my toes... in the roots of my hair. In that instant, I was convinced that we were both home, and no place else would ever compare to this.

Then he began to move. I could do nothing but hold on. I had no leverage in this position, with my shoulders pressed to the wall and my ankles crossed against the small of his back. I was sure it would have been completely impossible without the benefit of vampiric strength, but as it was, he lifted and lowered me in a powerful, rolling rhythm that built and built.

For all that I felt like I was being taken apart from the inside out and put back together piece by piece, this time I didn't feel the tightening coil that seemed to signify an approaching orgasm. Really, it was just as well, since I was pretty sure I'd pass out on the spot if I came with him inside me like this.

Better to hang on and enjoy the ride.

It was a good plan... or it would have been if my heart hadn't immediately insisted on getting involved in the action. Leonides' back was bowed, his face hidden against the juncture of my neck and shoulder as he rocked into me. The position muffled the small noises he was making. I couldn't tell if they signified pleasure or pain, and that was enough to have me wrapping around him even more tightly, erasing every millimeter of space between us.

"Shh," I murmured against his ear. "I'm here. We're both here, it's okay now."

He trembled, his movements losing rhythm. My heart clenched at the same time his body clenched, emptying into me. He was silent as he came, in counterpoint to my earlier caterwauling— which had no doubt been heard by every single person in the house. Later, that would probably bother me. Now, I put it out of my mind and clutched him to me, holding him close with all my strength.

Somehow, we ended up in a heap on the shower floor, water sluicing over us on its way to the drain. He was on his knees, and I was straddling his thighs, our arms wrapped around each other. His were trembling.

I still couldn't see a damned thing in the steamy dark.

As soon as either of us opened our mouths, we'd have to acknowledge what had just happened. So instead we huddled together, the silence broken only by the sound of water. I was aware of Leonides' release dripping out of me, only to be washed away. On some level, I was cognizant that I'd just let a man—well, a *vampire*—have unprotected sex with me.

But I had an IUD, and I'd been tested for sexually transmitted diseases before going to work for Guillermo. And as for Leonides... yeah, okay, he apparently had sex with a lot of women. I'd have to deal with that aspect later, though, because right now the water running over us was beginning to turn lukewarm. We'd almost exhausted whatever water heater was feeding it, and that meant we'd almost exhausted the amount of time we could stay like this without facing the rest of the world.

"I'm sorry." I felt the words against the side of my neck as much as I heard them. They were quiet. Hoarse. The voice didn't sound at all like Leonides' usual dark tones.

"For what?" I asked, after a confused beat.

But he only shook his head. At his gentle nudge, I climbed off him. He rose and helped me to my feet before turning off the water, just as it started to feel cold against my skin. I heard the shower door open, and felt his absence as he slipped out. A moment later, the bathroom lights flickered on. I blinked rapidly, only to be presented with a towel, which I took. Leonides didn't meet my gaze as he handed it to me.

Drying off was another way to put off the inevitable, so that's what we did. I took a step toward the vanity, only to wince as something small and hard dug into my bare heel. When I hopped back a step and looked down at the floor, it was to see one of the buttons that had popped off my borrowed shirt when Leonides had ripped it off me.

I wrapped the towel around my body and leaned down to pick it up. When I straightened, Leonides stood turned away from me, pulling his scrub pants over chiseled thighs and tight glutes. I retrieved Albigard's shirt and put it on. Somewhat to my surprise, it still had enough buttons attached to keep the front from gaping open. Then I steeled myself and met Leonides' eyes in the mirror.

"Sorry for what?" I repeated.

His expression was guarded. Only now, that blank wall looked as though the smallest impact might shatter it into crumbling shards.

"You drank succubus blood," he said. "Then, I drank your blood. And we fucked, despite the fact that you don't like sex, and I know better."

I stared at him for a few moments. "So… you didn't want to have sex?"

He stared back, through the medium of our reflections. "I—"

"Because, no offense, but you seemed pretty into it at the time," I continued.

"*We drank succubus blood*," he said again, like he thought I hadn't heard him the first time.

In my defense, I pondered the words for a bit before letting my inner bitch slip partly free of her chains.

"Oh," I said. "*Right*. Gotcha. Because clearly succubus blood overwhelms free will. Hmm. Guess I'll just pop downstairs and see if Rans and Zorah are up for a threesome, in that case." The look on his face morphed through *shocked* on its way to *scandalized* as I continued, "Or maybe Albigard, though he doesn't really seem like the type—"

"*Don't*." The tone of the word matched his earlier expression—hard, but in danger of cracking.

I clenched my jaw. "The point is, unless Zorah's blood hits vampires a hell of a lot harder than it hits witches, all it does is cause a minor distraction due to generalized horniness. So don't try to play this off as some kind of excuse why you weren't in your right mind, or something."

He held my gaze, unblinking. "Right. Because you would have done that in the normal course of things."

I didn't look away. "Well... I mean, *yeah*. I obviously would have. Is there really a question about that?"

His jaw ticked, and I was sure I wasn't imagining the haunted look in his brown eyes. "I wouldn't have."

And then he walked out of the bathroom.

FOURTEEN

I stood frozen in the steam-clouded bathroom, naked beneath a borrowed shirt with half its buttons ripped off. The hurt came first—lodging in my chest, predictable and unhelpful. It was replaced a moment later by anger, and finally, by a stubborn determination to have this out with him. *That* was something I could work with, so I stalked after Leonides, returning to the darkened bedroom.

I couldn't see him at first. If he'd dissolved into mist and flown away from me, I decided I was going straight back to anger, and screw maturity. After feeling my way around the room to the hallway door, I fumbled for the switch and turned the light on.

He hadn't left. He was standing at the window, his back to me. Apparently, we were going to have this conversation with all of our eye contact taking place via the medium of reflective surfaces.

"You're a filthy liar," I told him.

"Yes," he agreed. "About so many things. But not about this."

"Bullcrap, Mr. 'Sex Doesn't Have to Mean Anything,'" I said.

He was silent. It looked like we'd be doing this the hard way, then.

"So," I pressed on, "since we both know perfectly well that you didn't magically lose control of your dick just because you downed a few cc's of second-hand succubus blood, the question becomes... *why* are you lying?"

The tendon at the corner of his jaw ticked. I let the silence stretch, to see if I could wait him out. It admittedly wasn't a strategy I'd had much luck with in the past, but right now I was feeling pretty damned motivated. The atmosphere on his side grew thick with unspoken words until I imagined I could almost feel the shape of them.

"*I can't save you*, Vonnie," he said, biting it off angrily.

And... *nope*. Not what I'd expected, no clue where that had come from, or what I was supposed to do with it.

"Did I ask you to?" I asked, more than a little bewildered. After a beat, I added, "And that has *what* to do with the sex, exactly?"

"I can't save anyone," he continued. "I told you up front, just because I take in strays, it doesn't mean I'm a safe person to be around. If today didn't manage to drive that point home—"

"You saved Zorah," I interrupted. "When you were running from the Fae, when she almost died—you saved her by turning her into a vampire."

His voice was tight. "She's bound to Nigellus, through her life-bond with Rans. The damned demon would have brought her back regardless... and *he* wouldn't have left her a vampire afterward."

"You saved Len," I said. "When Kat's ex put a knife through his lung."

"An ambulance crew could've done the same thing."

"You saved Albigard," I went on inexorably. "In Dhuinne."

"The fuck I did. *You* saved Albigard, and now you're his personal fuel cell anytime he needs to draw power from someone."

I took a deep breath, aware that I was entering dangerous waters. "You saved your wife."

His hands landed heavily on the windowsill, as though he suddenly needed it to hold himself up.

"No," he rasped. "I didn't."

I sat on the edge of the bed, cut down at the knees by the pain in that normally even voice. "Tell me," I ordered. "Leonides, for god's sake… *tell me what happened.*"

Silence descended over the room once more, lasting long enough that I wasn't sure he would answer. I also wasn't sure what to do next, if he didn't. I *couldn't* let this go. Not now. Not after everything that had happened today.

When he finally spoke, the words were barely audible.

"Once upon a time, I was a sniper in the 370th Regimental Combat Team in Italy, during the Second World War," he said. "After the war ended, I came back to the States, and got out of the army a few years later. Clarabelle had been my high school sweetheart, and she'd waited for me. We got married. I eventually managed to get a foot in the door with the first black-owned securities firm in the U.S.—a place called McGhee & Company, located in Cleveland."

It was still difficult to wrap my mind around Leonides' true age, and yet this unexpected glimpse into his past held me rapt.

"Times were hard, but the future was looking pretty good for us, all things considered," he continued. "Right up until Clarabelle visited a doctor to find out why she hadn't gotten pregnant, even though we'd been trying for months. He found a tumor growing in her breast. It turned out to be cancerous."

I nodded, already aware of this part of the story, at least in broad strokes.

"Surgery and radiation were the treatments of the day, but they didn't usually work. I begged her to try them anyway." He swallowed. "I didn't tell her how fast the bills were likely to bankrupt us, though. Within a few months, we were just about broke, and she was too sick to leave the hospital."

"And that's when you met the demon?" I asked.

His shoulders curved inward. "Yeah. I have no idea what brought me to Myrial's attention, but just when things were at their darkest, this rich white guy shows up and offers me a bargain—my soul in exchange for Clarabelle's cancer going into remission."

I couldn't even conceive of what that must have been like.

"Did you know what you were really getting into?" I asked, trying to imagine how I'd react if

Nigellus popped in right now and offered Jace's safe return in exchange for my soul. "Did you know Myrial was a demon?"

He snorted. "Oh, yeah. Of course I did. And I jumped on that deal like a hungry cat pouncing on a mouse." His chest rose and fell. "Within a matter of days, Clarabelle started getting stronger. The tumor began to shrink, and within a couple of months it was too small to be detectable at all."

This was the part I already knew about, but there had to be more.

"Something else happened, though," I said.

His hands clenched the edges of the window-sill harder. "Of course it fucking did. Four months after her recovery, she went out to the corner store in broad daylight one afternoon. A drunk driver mounted the sidewalk and ran her over. She died right there on the side of the road, and I've missed her every goddamned day since. When the police showed up at the office to tell me what had happened, it felt like my heart was being cut out of my chest. Almost seventy years later, the hole's still there."

My eyes slid closed, tears burning hot behind them for this man who'd carried his pain around in a box for a lifetime and then some.

"I'm so sorry," I said, painfully aware of the words' inadequacy. "She must have been an amazing person."

I heard him swallow. "She was a middle class woman from a poor family, who never finished high school or worked outside the home. And when she smiled," — his voice wavered on the word — "it lit up an entire city block."

I had to swallow, too, before I could be sure of my voice. "And would she want you to be alone forever? Or would she want you to remember the good times, and move on?"

"I don't know," he replied to the window. "She's dead, so it's not like I can really ask her." His shoulders hitched, and he made a sound like a rusty hinge. It was the least laughter-like laugh I'd ever heard someone produce. "Besides, I don't need to ask her. The choices I've made since she's been gone have always been my call, not hers. And twenty years later, that was exactly what I told myself when this high-powered businesswoman set her sights on me and convinced me maybe I should give love another try. *'Clarabelle would want me to have this,'* I told myself."

I frowned, a niggle of disquiet pricking at me.

"This woman was mesmerizing," he went on. "Made me feel like I was the center of the universe... like maybe I could have a future beyond making an endless supply of money for the demon I'd sold my soul to."

He made the harsh, not-laughing sound again. "I might've felt a bit different about things if I'd realized it was the same goddamned demon, only in female form — fucking me over again, this time literally."

Mental connections clicked into place. "Zorah's demon..." I murmured. "She said the demon who got her grandmother pregnant stole your DNA to do it."

"A fact I only learned fifty years later," he said dully. "Long after my daughter was dead from an assassin's bullet. The only daughter I'll ever have, now."

"But still in time to know your granddaughter," I pointed out. "Your granddaughter... who's pretty freaking awesome. And who loves you. Zorah thinks you hung the stars in the sky."

He loosed one hand from its grip on the windowsill to run it over his face. "I know. It's just... I'm so damned tired, Vonnie. And until some monster manages to chop my head off or run silver through my heart properly, it's *never going to end*."

I stared at his back. "You're an idiot."

He turned and met my eyes directly for the first time since I'd followed him into the bedroom. "Yeah? Go on. Tell me something I *don't* know."

But I waved him down. "No, stop that. You're an idiot because whether you have sex with someone or not makes no difference to how you feel about them."

He raised an eyebrow at me. "No offense, but that's supposed to be my line. And I think we've already established that you've been having the wrong kind of sex for the last fifteen years."

I gave him a look that clearly said, *'Really?'* and pointed at the bathroom. "Stop deflecting." I jabbed my finger, indicating the offending shower stall. "Because that? *That* was a symptom, not a cause."

He didn't look impressed. "And yet, I still can't give you what you need."

I probably didn't look too impressed, either. "You think not? Because what I need is you here, helping. I might also need more of your blood at some point, though honestly Rans and Zorah's packs more of a punch."

"I'd noticed," he deadpanned.

"And frankly?" I continued, ignoring the interruption. "The sex was really nice, but I can live without it. I've kind of got more important things on my mind right now, succubus blood or no."

"Good call, that."

Jesus. He still wasn't getting it, and I didn't have the energy to perform any more emotional labor for him right now.

I sighed, giving up for the moment and switching gears. "Look. Stay here for a minute. I'll be right back, and I promise to shut up about it, at least for tonight. I... had Rans pick up a couple of things for you while he was out."

His brows drew together in confusion. "What kind of things?" He sounded as tired as I felt.

"A crochet hook and some loc butter," I told him. "Because I'm sorry, but your hair is driving me insane."

I left him frowning after me, and went back to my room to get the aforementioned items, along with a comb and the wooden chair, since there hadn't been a chair in Leonides' borrowed room. When I returned, he was still staring at the doorway with a furrowed brow.

I plopped the chair down beneath the overhead light fixture, facing the bedroom mirror.

"Instant locs. I can't sleep, so you're getting some. Sit."

He didn't move. And, to be fair, I guess that *did* deserve a bit more explanation from the ginger-haired white girl.

"Look, we lived next door to a Black family when I was growing up. Mom didn't like it when the kids and I played together, but there weren't any other children our age in the neighborhood, so we did it anyway. When I was fourteen, I learned how to do dreadlocks for them. Well... one kind, anyway. The fast kind." I brandished the crochet hook in its plastic package, wiggling it back and forth.

"Okay. That, I'll admit I did not see coming," he said.

I shrugged. "Yeah, yeah. Look at me, busting the stereotypes. I can't sleep anyway, and there's no TV or internet in this place. Your dreads were pretty thick before, so there won't be a gazillion of them. Just be glad you didn't wear your hair in braids or cornrows. I'd have no clue on that."

He shook his head, as though trying to catalogue this unexpected piece of information.

"Am I going to have to drag you into this chair by the scruff?" I asked, my patience wearing thin. "Because it's late, and yesterday was one of the worst days of my life, and I'd really like to lose myself in something mindless and comforting for a while. Something besides sex, I mean."

He made another barely audible choked noise.

I pointed at the chair. "Sit. Down. *Seriously.*"

Somewhat to my surprise, Leonides crossed the room and sat. The same dazed, distant look from earlier dulled his gaze as he stared at his own reflection. I felt a similar reaction, like a weight in my chest—the events of the last twelve hours clamoring for my attention. Shoving it all aside, I set the comb and crochet hook on the dresser.

After breaking the plastic seal on the loc butter, I scooped some up and set the container to the side. It was a relief to get my hands in Leonides' hair, shifting my focus from the cerebral to the tactile. Maybe I wasn't alone. As soon as he was sure I wasn't going to make him talk about emotions again, his eyes slipped shut. I massaged the shea butter into his scalp, working my fingers through the rat's nest of kinky tangles.

I lost myself in the mindlessness of it, conditioning and detangling, first by hand, and then with the comb. By the time I was done, his hair was dry enough to section, and some of the tension had drained out of his shoulders. I glanced at his face in the mirror, only to find his eyes still closed.

It had been a while since I was fourteen, giggling with Chantelle and Nyah as we tried to keep the parts straight. I had to backtrack a few times to make sure the sections were even and not too small, twisting each bunch of hair with the comb to keep it separated while I worked.

"Should've had Rans get some gel, too," I muttered.

Leonides snorted. "The vain English prat probably has some in his luggage. You've seen his hair."

It was the first hint of humor I'd heard from him since… well, *since.* A small smile tugged at one corner of my lips. "Eh, I think you're okay without. It might speed things up a bit on the front end, but it'll just make white flakes when it dries."

We fell back into silence, though it felt easier than before. Eventually, I managed to get his hair sectioned and twisted to my satisfaction, at which point I tore open the package containing the crochet hook.

"How did you have these done before?" I asked curiously.

"Braids plus time," he said, still not opening his eyes. "Definitely no arts and crafts supplies involved."

"Oy. Respect the instant locs," I said, mocksternly. Keeping things light. "Like I said, it's the only kind I ever learned how to do. And besides, this way you can take a miss on the ugly inbetween stage."

Starting at the top of his forehead, I grasped a twist of hair by the end and slid the crochet tool through the hair near the scalp, hooking a few strands from the outside of the twist and pulling them to the inside. It didn't take long for muscle memory to reawaken, the repetitive motion becoming almost hypnotic as my speed and confidence increased.

Work from the top to the bottom. Twist the dread as you go to make sure it's evenly locked along the short length. Change the angle of the crochet hook to pull the loose ends into the body and keep it from unraveling. Pull the finished dread through its own base—first from one side, then from the other side, and finally from top to bottom so it would lie flat.

Hours passed, my fingers aching but my mind blissfully blank, focused only on the task at hand. Leonides sat motionless in the chair, his head tipped forward to give me access to the final row at the nape of his neck. Eventually, I settled the last dread into place, feeling thrown for a moment when I realized there was nothing left to do. I glanced up, looking at his reflection, my vision wavering as sudden exhaustion overcame me.

"All done," I whispered.

He lifted his head, his deep brown eyes opening... staring at his reflection blankly. A hand lifted, carding through the short dreadlocks.

I swallowed. "I think they were thicker before," I said.

"No," he said quietly. "This is great. Thank you, Vonnie."

Suddenly, the thought of walking back to my room at the other end of the floor felt overwhelming, and I sagged a bit. "God, I'm fucking exhausted," I murmured, bracing a hand on the chair back.

"I can't imagine why," he said, laying on the irony. "Come on. You might as well just crash here. It's not like it's the first time."

Tomorrow, I would beat myself up for falling into bed with the guy who'd just cut me off at the knees after having sex with me. Now, relief hit me so intensely that I swayed.

"Okay," I said, and let him take the crochet needle from my hand.

A moment later, I was under the covers, blinking up at him—at the incontrovertible proof that somehow, we'd managed to save him. He was here. He was okay. Leonides turned off the light and settled on top of the covers next to me, which was probably ridiculous at this point. I fumbled blindly for his arm, surrendering to some deep-seated need to feel his cool skin beneath my touch as I fell asleep. Even with my eyelids sliding closed, I got the sense that he was looking down at me… watching me intently.

That's right, I thought disjointedly. *See me. I'm right here. I'm not going to run.*

The question was, would he?

FIFTEEN

"Up and at 'em, you two!" Rans' overly cheerful voice pierced the heavy veil of sleep and jerked me back to reluctant wakefulness. I groaned in dismay and pressed my face more fully into the form I was lying against. The... *person* I was lying against.

I froze, casting my muddled brain back to the last thing I could remember.

"Rans," Leonides said, "you are such an unmitigated asshole sometimes."

"Nonsense," Rans replied briskly. "Would you rather sleep through our meeting with the lads at the *Weekly Oracle* in a couple of hours? Love the hair, by the way. I was really hoping we weren't going to end up revisiting the late seventies 'giant afro' phase."

"Get out," Leonides told him in a tired tone.

"Whatever you say, mate," Rans said. "Vonnie, there's food downstairs. We need to leave in ninety minutes."

The door closed softly, and I felt Leonides' chest lift and lower in a sigh. At that point, there was really nothing to do except roll onto my back and face the music.

"Well," I rasped, my voice sleep-heavy. "This is awkward. *Again.*"

He was silent for a moment before replying.

"Just as well we have other things to worry about. For now, let's focus on that."

"'Kay," I said, accepting the lifeline. Even so, I couldn't stop myself from asking, "How are you this morning, though? Did you sleep?"

"A bit," he replied, pointedly ignoring the first question. "You?"

I took stock. The results were... not great. "Um..."

He nodded. "Yesterday wasn't something you shake off with a few hours' sleep. You should probably eat something."

I blinked at the ceiling. "As long as Rans picked up coffee when he was doing the grocery run."

"If he hasn't learned *that* lesson in seven hundred years among humans, then he really *is* an asshole," Leonides said, before rolling out of the bed.

I took a moment to drink in the sight of him, unable to stop myself. He looked... fine. Exactly the same as he always had, with the exception of a subtle difference in hairstyle.

"I'm glad we got you out of there," I blurted out of the blue, and then silently cursed myself.

Smooth. Real smooth.

He paused, his back to me. "I'm... sorry you had to see me like that. And I'm glad you and Zorah are all right."

Level. Controlled. And oh-so-carefully phrased. I took a deep breath and let it go, because I couldn't play full-time armchair psychologist for a

man in pain while also trying to save the world —
and more specifically, trying to save my son.

"I'll go get cleaned up and see you downstairs," I told him. "There's clothes and stuff for
you in the hall by the door."

And then I left the room, my mind whirling.

Back in my suite, I showered mechanically, not
allowing myself to think about the last shower I'd
had. The availability of shampoo and conditioner
felt like untold luxury. Too bad I'd accidentally left
my comb on Leonides' dresser, covered with shea
butter. I dried off in front of the dusty mirror,
dressed in black leggings and a t-shirt, and finger-
combed my hair into a semblance of order.

Downstairs, there was — thankfully — coffee.
Also orange juice and Danish, along with ham,
bread, and pre-packaged hard-boiled eggs. I was
alone in the dining room for the first few minutes,
but Zorah joined me as I was pouring a third cup of
coffee.

She sat across from me, resting her chin on a
cupped hand and staring at me. I felt the blush
crawl up my neck, and swallowed a bite of Danish.

"What?" I asked, not able to stifle the hint of
belligerence in my tone.

She shook her head at me slowly. "The walls
here aren't that thick, babe. So, am I going to need
to start calling you Step-Grandma anytime soon?"

I groaned and shoved my paper plate out of
the way, so I could let my head fall forward onto
the table dramatically. "Stop. *Seriously*. Because this
isn't so much a relationship as a really hot mistake I
keep making," I told the chipped linoleum.

"Yeah… no," Zorah said. "Trust me, babe. It's a relationship. You two just haven't realized it yet."

"If you say so," I mumbled, not raising my head. Eventually, I peeked up at her through a curtain of messy red hair. "Let's just say that between the two of us, there's a fair amount of baggage involved. And I don't really have the emotional energy to spare at the moment, you know what I mean?"

She pushed her chair back from the table and came around to my side, where she draped an arm across my bowed shoulders and dropped a kiss on the top of my head.

"Fair," she said.

I dragged myself upright so I could twist around and turn it into a proper hug. She gave a light squeeze and let go.

"It's funny," she continued. "This is giving me a fresh appreciation for what Rans must have gone through before I finally pulled my head out of my ass and got over myself."

"Oh, you've no idea," said a cultured English voice from the doorway. "Torture, it was — like having toenails pulled out by the root. Took me right back to the Middle Ages."

He sauntered over and drew Zorah against him for a peck on the cheek.

"Dick," she murmured fondly.

Rans gave her a look equally as fond, and the brief exchange shouldn't have ached in my chest like it did. When he turned his attention to me, I consciously squared my shoulders.

His blue eyes held understanding... perhaps even sympathy. "To everything there is a season, Vonnie—and a time to every purpose under heaven. Right now, our purpose is to find answers, and to that end, I believe it's in our best interest to think laterally."

I nodded. "You think these... underground newspaper people might help with some of those answers? How?"

Zorah retook her seat and leaned forward, elbows on the table. "You remember I told you they were big into ghost hunting... EMF detection, that kind of stuff?"

I rubbed at my temples. "Please don't tell me ghosts are a real thing. I'm having enough trouble keeping up as it is."

Leonides and Albigard chose that moment to join us in the dining room.

"Ghosts are not, in fact, a *thing*," Rans assured me. "But changes in the ether—in the electromagnetic field, if you prefer—very much are."

"So these guys are like the blind men describing an elephant?" Leonides offered. I glanced over at him, and was almost surprised when he met my gaze rather than avoiding it.

"Well put," Rans said. "That's precisely it. One man believes he's touching a rope. Another, a python. Another, a tree trunk. And another, a solid wall. But in reality, all of them are seeing Fae activity along the ley lines."

"Okay, I suppose that's one way to torture a metaphor," Zorah observed. "Seriously, though, we used their data once before—to figure out that my father had been taken to the gateway in County Meath. It's worth checking to see if they can help us with this, too."

I turned to address Albigard, who had remained silent so far. "So, if the Unseelie have been taking children somewhere on Earth and hiding them, they'll have been using these… ley lines?"

"Yes," he said simply.

"The problem is," Rans put in, "it's a big planet. And I can guarantee the Fae aren't holding a large group of kidnapped magical children in Chicago. We need access to the conspiracy theorists' network of like-minded researchers across the globe."

Zorah nodded. "Right. These guys are all about internet forums and data-sharing. I used to hang out on the fringes of that world, back when I was young and trying to make sense of my mother's death."

"It's true. You should ask her what her username used to be, sometime," Rans said, as an aside.

Zorah smacked him in the ribs, but ignored him otherwise. "Anyway, we're after whatever information they can provide regarding worldwide EMF hotspots. With luck, we'll be able to use the information to narrow things down."

I nodded and retrieved my abandoned coffee, which had grown lukewarm as we talked. "Okay, it certainly sounds like more of a plan than what we've been stumbling around with so far." Knocking back the tepid caffeine, I met Albigard's green eyes. "Sure you can't offer any more insight, here?"

He lifted a shoulder and let it drop. "The location will presumably be somewhere remote and lightly populated. Possibly *un*populated — though if so, it would have to be someplace with an extremely accommodating climate. Beyond that, you already have all the information I possess."

I nodded thoughtfully and tackled the rest of the Danish. Unfortunately, I suspected there were any number of places around the world that would fit the bill. Something about that realization made me feel very far away from Jace.

"When do we leave for this meeting?" I asked. "And how are we getting there?"

"Whenever you're done," Rans said easily. "And by pimpmobile, of course."

SIXTEEN

We piled into the old Lincoln Continental— with the exception of Albigard, who was supposed to be in hiding anyway. Zorah called shotgun while Rans drove, leaving me in the back seat with Leonides. He looked around the interior with something approaching dismay, and I wondered how long it had been since the last time he'd ridden in a vehicle that cost less than my annual salary.

"Good god," he said. "This is even worse than I'd imagined—and that's saying something."

"The engine runs," Rans replied dryly, easing the mechanical beast down a long, winding driveway. "And really, Guthrie—it's not appreciably worse than that old Ford Thunderbird you used to drive, back when Nixon was president."

"Hold your heathen tongue," Leonides said, in a tone of offense. "The *hell* it's not."

I made a dedicated attempt to put aside the weirdness of discussing Nixon's presidency as though it were something that had happened in recent memory. Instead, I allowed myself to feel relief at the return of a degree of normalcy after yesterday's nightmare. We'd survived. Leonides and Rans were bantering about cars. We were taking action that might even yield some kind of measurable result.

Things could be worse.

"Did you get hold of Len last night?" I asked, hoping that we hadn't put him through yet more trauma when the building explosion made the six-o'clock news.

"I did," Rans replied. "He agreed — reluctantly — to deny any knowledge regarding your survival or lack thereof. The longer we can keep the Fae guessing as to whether you and Guthrie made it out, the better."

Even with Len in the loop, it was bad enough that Kat, Maurice, and our other coworkers might assume we were dead. But that assumption would probably keep them safer.

"Makes sense," I allowed, leaning back in the seat to watch our surroundings go by.

Oddly, I'd never been to Chicago until now, despite the fact that it was a common weekend getaway for St. Louisans. I'd gotten a glimpse of the iconic skyline as we drove east from wherever Albigard's safehouse was located. Once inside the city, Rans navigated us along an increasingly confusing route, our surroundings growing noticeably shabbier the farther we went.

The *Weekly Oracle* was located on a block that reminded me quite a bit of the down-at-heels neighborhood where Richard's smoke shop had been. Buildings that had once housed offices and apartments now stood largely vacant, with many of the windows boarded up and trash along the edges of the road.

"This sure brings back memories," Zorah said. "You take me to all the nicest places, lover."

"Hmm. Mostly, I'm just curious to see if you intend to drool all over Derrick again," Rans replied, amusement clear in his tone.

Zorah sighed. "Ha, ha. You're just jealous because you lack his internet cred." She had pity on us in the back seat. "Derrick Nicolaev is one of the owners of the paper. Back in the day, he was a pretty big deal online. We had a few exchanges in one of the larger paranormal and conspiracy forums when I was, like, sixteen. He went by Hypnos on the net, and I had no idea it was the same guy when we first came here. I… might've had a bit of a fangirl moment when I finally realized."

"This is the part where someone asks her about her username," Rans added helpfully.

"No," Zorah said flatly, glaring daggers at him. "It's really not."

Leonides appeared to share my general sense of bewilderment, but Rans had pity on her and let it go as he turned his attention to parking. The car doors squeaked in painful protest as we got out, and Rans led us to a nondescript building boasting more intact glass and less plywood than some of its neighbors. The underground newspaper was — you guessed it — underground, in the basement. Rans opened a door with a faded sign hanging over it and held it for us, gesturing us past him. Once inside, we trooped down a concrete stairwell to the lower level.

The stairs were dimly lit after the glare outside, and I had to fight a spasm of irrational panic as my mind flashed back to the explosion in Leonides' building. I shut my eyes tightly for a moment and breathed. I would *not* end up with a fear of basements, or stairwells, or tall buildings, or any of the other crap my stupid brain tried to insist was dangerous.

"All right?" Leonides' quiet voice in my ear made me jump, my nerves on edge.

"Yeah, fine," I said quickly. Geez... he'd probably heard my heart rate increase or something. "Just... the last time we were in a basement, it didn't go so well."

"Right," he said. "Frankly, I'm glad I don't remember much between sending you off with Zorah and waking up in Albigard's kitchen."

Something eased inside me upon learning that he hadn't been conscious for every moment of agony as his body burned.

"Trust me," I whispered, "you didn't miss anything important."

I straightened my spine and continued down the steps toward the newspaper's offices, my eyes adjusting after a few seconds. The home of the *Weekly Oracle* was a large, mostly unfinished space with the clattering sound of machinery emerging from its depths. Again, I pushed aside the associations with the mechanical HVAC floor in Guthrie's building in favor of looking around the place.

A large reception desk dominated the front area, with the real work apparently taking place in the back. A maze of beige cubicle walls divided the rear area into different sections, several of which boasted messy desks covered with a combination of aging computer technology and takeout boxes. Bundled cables and wires snaked along the floor.

"Hullo!" Rans called briskly, stopping in front of the reception desk and leaning an elbow on it.

"Hang on!" replied a voice from the depths of the cavernous space. "With you in a minute!"

We waited, and in due course movement in the back resolved itself into a blond man in his late twenties, wearing glasses. He made his way to the front, his gray gaze flickering over us in that vaguely nervous way common to the chronically shy.

"Hey there," he said, shooting Zorah a quick smile. "Well, if it isn't *TeamEdward4eva* in the flesh. Catch any ghosts lately?"

Despite the grimness of everything that had happened, I choked on a snort of laughter as the connection slipped into place. Zorah's username, outing her as a closet teenage *Twilight* fan. No wonder Rans gave her a hard time about it.

"Not recently, *Hypnos*," she replied, though not before casting me a dirty look. "Thought maybe you and the others could help us out with that today."

'Hypnos' shot us another look, this one laced with curiosity. Rans straightened. "Right. Sorry. Derrick, this is Guthrie and Vonnie. Guthrie and Vonnie... Derrick. We're here today because we have reason to believe there's been a large concentration of EMF activity along the ley lines recently, and we need to pinpoint where it is."

Derrick frowned. "I dunno, man. It's actually been pretty quiet around here for the past few months. What kind of time frame are we talking about?"

"Ah," Rans said. "There's the rub. We're not talking about a *local* concentration, you see. This will almost certainly be somewhere remote. And I mean that in a worldwide sense, not just a North American sense."

"Can you help us?" I asked, suddenly desperate to know whether I dared get my hopes up.

Derrick looked taken aback. "Well... you know, we're not a big operation here. We lay out some detection equipment near local hotspots—northern Illinois and Indiana, sometimes a bit farther afield if the data is interesting. But that's about it. Anything more, and we don't have the manpower to maintain it or keep track of the readings."

Zorah leaned forward. "We're after your connections more than we're after your readings on this one. You're still in contact with other people doing the same kind of thing, but in different parts of the world, right?"

He shrugged. "Yeah, we are. But it's not as though there's some overarching global organization for this stuff. These days, it's just a bunch of conspiracy geeks chatting on NorChan, really."

"That's exactly what we need," Leonides said. "Someone who knows where to look and who to talk to about any concentration of activity over the past several weeks."

"Okay. Fair enough," Derrick said. "Isaac's out on a delivery run right now, and Óliver went to get takeout. I can get on the boards and start poking around until they get back to help. You four gonna hang out here for a bit?"

"If it won't be an intrusion," Rans said.

Derrick only shook his head. "No, man. Better if you're here to answer any questions that might come up." He gave Rans and Zorah an assessing look. "Speaking of which, you never did say what your theory about the EMF spike was, the last time you were here. Care to share?"

Rans hesitated for the barest moment before replying. "Not sunspots, I'm afraid."

Derrick waved the words away. "Yeah, yeah. We disproved that one pretty thoroughly over the winter. Come on. Spill. It can't be any weirder than Isaac's ideas about the Illuminati."

Again, the slightest pause.

"There's some evidence that the ley line activity is tied to abductions of a... non-terrestrial variety," Rans told him.

If I expected laughter or eye-rolling, all I got was a thoughtful noise.

"Huh," Derrick said. "Well, I can't say it's the first time I've heard someone float that theory. There was a guy a few years back who claimed UFOs were using the ley lines to navigate, but he got hounded off the forum by the ghost-chasers." He frowned. "Out of curiosity, what sent you down that path? It's not an angle you hear many people talking about."

I swallowed. "My son's been taken. We're trying to find him."

He went still. "Oh. Oh, shit."

Should I have told him that? Whatever the case, Zorah immediately ran with it.

"He disappeared from a commercial passenger jet in mid-air," she said. "He was on board when it took off, but not when it touched down. The authorities have been suppressing the story."

"Holy crap," Derrick said, apparently not questioning the unlikely sounding tale. "Any chance the plane landed somewhere along the way? Secretly, I mean?"

"There wasn't time for an extra stopover," Leonides offered. "It arrived at the scheduled destination a few minutes early."

"And it was very definitely the right plane," Rans put in. "We've already been to both ends of the route to investigate that aspect directly."

Derrick shook his head as if to clear it. "This is... wow. Okay, let me think. What was the route? That seems like the place to start looking for anomalies."

"Denver to El Paso," I told him.

"But that's not the approach we need to take," Rans said firmly. "There are a number of related disappearances across the globe. We're looking for the place they converge, not the places they originate."

"Somewhere lightly populated, or maybe even uninhabited," I added, echoing what Albigard had said. "Somewhere remote."

Derrick blinked behind his glasses. "So you think they're still on Earth, at least. That's... good, right?"

"Better than the alternative, certainly," Zorah said.

"Right. So we need a remote location on a convergence of ley lines that's seen unusual EMF activity over the past weeks or months," Derrick summarized. "Gotcha."

The stairwell door opened, and a tough-looking Latino guy carrying a brown paper sack walked in. His brown eyes played over us, as if he was assessing our potential threat level. After a moment, his attention moved to Derrick.

"They were out of mango rice," he said without preliminaries, just as the distinctive smell of Thai carryout reached me. He set down the bag, and my eyes were drawn to the empty left sleeve of his jacket.

"Hey, Óliver," Derrick greeted. "You remember these two, right?" He gestured to Rans and Zorah. "They need access to worldwide data on ley line EMF activity concentrated in remote locations. Any ideas?"

A few minutes after that, the last member of the Weekly Oracle staff wandered in — a red-haired kid named Isaac who looked like he should be on a college football team somewhere, rather than delivering copies of an obscure conspiracy rag to newsstands around Chicago. After everyone had been brought up to speed, we retired to the warren of cubicle walls and cooled our heels while the three guys tapped rapidly on computer keyboards while intermittently slurping noodles.

"Other users want to know why we're asking," Isaac said. "Should we tell them?"

"Best not," Rans advised. "It's clear the powers that be want to keep this quiet, and there's no telling where they've got moles planted."

Part of me wanted to scream the entire story to the skies and make as big a stink as possible. But I'd already seen far too clearly what could happen when innocent people ended up caught in the Fae's crosshairs. Case in point—I should probably take this chance to check the news on my phone, and see if a death count had been released after the explosion in St. Louis yesterday.

I didn't look.

The *Weekly Oracle* guys threw occasional snippets of conversation back and forth, but other than that, the time dragged as they trawled through whatever sources of data were available. Eventually, Derrick sat up from his keyboard hunch and pushed back from his desk with a sigh.

"So, here's the problem," he said. "By definition, if a place is remote, you don't get a lot of people going there and setting up ghost detection equipment. Know what I mean?"

The weight of fading hope settled across my shoulders.

"Unfortunately, that makes perfect sense," Zorah said, sounding just as disappointed.

"Then we need to look at this from another direction," Leonides stated flatly. "Can we start simple, and list remote areas that also have an intersection of ley lines?"

Óliver shrugged. "Don't see why not. Are we talking 'a few miles to the nearest city' levels of remote, or 'the expedition we sent there in nineteen-eighty never returned' levels of remote?"

"Somewhere between the two, at a guess," Rans said. "Though probably closer to the latter than the former."

Isaac blew out a breath. "We can start with the really out-there places, and get less picky later if we need to."

"Sounds reasonable," Derrick said. "Tell you what. This is going to take a while—probably the rest of the day. Can I email you the results when we've got them? No point in you being stuck here the whole time."

"I'm afraid we're somewhat technologically challenged at the moment," Rans told him, "Why don't we swing by tomorrow morning and discuss the results in person?"

"That works, too," Derrick said. His gray, bespectacled gaze fell on me with unexpected forthrightness. "We'll put all our focus on it. I can't guarantee we'll find anything useful, but it won't be for lack of trying."

The backs of my eyes burned, and I had to swallow before I could reply. "Thanks—all of you. That means a lot to me right now."

Derrick nodded, shooting me a small, crooked smile that didn't reach his eyes.

SEVENTEEN

We drove back to the suburbs, where Albigard's warded house stood on a tree-lined slope. I had to blink rapidly as Rans turned the pimpmobile into the driveway, because I would have sworn there was nothing there—no opening in the trees, no graveled drive.

"Fucking David Copperfield bullshit," Leonides muttered next to me, and I gathered this must be the outward manifestation of the protective magic surrounding the property. Like my concealed necklace, but on a much larger scale.

"Just be glad Tinkerbell opened the wards to me when we arrived yesterday," Rans shot back. "Otherwise, this might have been awkward."

I had a brief flash of the four of us driving randomly up and down the street in search of a driveway none of us could see, and silently agreed with the assessment. Once we'd parked and approached the door, Rans knocked rather than going straight in.

"We're back. Invite them in, why don't you," he said, when Albigard opened the door.

"Of course," said the Fae. His eyes skimmed over each of us, one by one. "Enter. You are all welcome here. Did you find what you needed?"

I felt a shiver of magic wash over me as the wards accepted us, and rubbed at my arms as though to warm them. "Not yet. We're going back tomorrow, in hopes that they'll have gathered more information by then."

He tipped his head in acknowledgement and stood aside for us to enter, locking the door behind us.

"I desperately need lunch and a nap, unless there's something productive I can do," I told the others.

"No, get some rest," Zorah said. "We all should, while we're waiting for news."

So, for lack of anything else to do, I ate a sandwich and crashed in my borrowed room for a bit—tired enough by this point that insomnia wasn't an issue.

Zorah woke me as the sun was slipping low in the sky. "Hey, babe—we're going into the city for a few hours to feed. I figure it's best for us to be maxed out on power in preparation for whatever our next step ends up being. One of us can squeeze you out some vampire juice when we get back, okay?"

"Yeah, okay," I said groggily. "Thanks."

She left, and I hauled myself out of bed, knowing I'd be awake half the night if I didn't get up. When I stumbled down to the kitchen, it was to find Leonides and Albigard chatting in quiet tones as the Fae sliced an apple over the sink with a wicked-looking dagger, eating the pieces one by one.

I looked at Leonides curiously. "I figured you'd be out with the rest of the fang brigade."

"Grabbing a bite, you mean?" he asked dryly.

I shrugged. "Hey... you said it, not me."

"I'm headed out shortly. 'Feeding' means something a bit different to a succubus than to a regular vampire. I'm more than happy to leave that aspect of things well alone."

Albigard snorted around his slice of apple.

"Gotcha," I said. "So, Albigard—if we're going to be stuck here on our own for a bit, can we talk about magic? Edward started me out with the basics, but I suspect anything else I can learn about it may end up being useful."

The Fae eyed me up and down. "As you like, adept. I have no other pressing engagements, as you can see."

"Great." I rummaged in the fridge and made myself another sandwich, watching Albigard grazing on fruit out of the corner of my eye. Finally, curiosity overcame me. "So, are you a vegetarian, then?"

He raised an eyebrow. "Hardly. I merely prefer meat that's been hunted, rather than meat that's been raised in a cage and fed swill all its life."

"I had an uncle you probably would have liked," I told him.

"Doubtful," he retorted.

"On that note," Leonides said, "I guess I'll leave you both to it. Try not to destroy anything while we're gone."

I shot him a flat stare.

Albigard flicked his fingers in a dismissive gesture. Once Leonides left, I devoted myself to my ham sandwich, finding the presence of someone who had no real desire to converse with me surprisingly soothing.

"Come," the Fae said, once we were both finished eating. "I tire of the indoors."

It was blustery outside, but not too uncomfortable. I followed Albigard farther up the slope on which the house was built, until he stopped near a jutting gray rock and lowered himself to sit cross-legged on the ground. The rock was big and flat enough for me to perch on, so I did. The property was hopelessly overgrown, and for a few moments, we just looked out over the trees while the evening dusk grew deeper. I wondered if Albigard had purposely left the place this way to make it seem more like Dhuinne.

"You expressed interest in the theory that human magic is descended from Fae magic," he said eventually, surprising me by breaking the silence.

"Yes," I said simply. When he didn't immediately continue, I took a deep breath and asked the first of the questions I'd been wondering about. "Does Fae elemental magic work the same way as human magic? Is it tied to your emotions?"

Albigard looked thoughtful. "I would not have described it in such a way, no. One controls the elements by sensing them through the magical field, and altering that field."

"Huh," I mused. "Yeah, that's not been my experience of it at all. Though I suppose I can sense something you might call a 'field' through my pendant when I concentrate. Next question — why is it that you can control elements here on Earth, when I couldn't affect elements in Dhuinne at all?"

He huffed out a breath. "Because elements in Dhuinne are far more challenging to control."

I digested that. "So, if you're strong enough to affect things in Dhuinne, Earth elements aren't a challenge? If I were more powerful, would I eventually be able to control elements in Dhuinne?"

Albigard shrugged. "I cannot say. It's possible that human magic is simply too different to work in the Fae realm. Or perhaps you could manage it, with enough raw magical power."

I tilted my head at him. "Since you can pull power from me, does that mean I can pull power from you?"

His lips pulled into a smile. It wasn't a nice expression. "No."

That had been a bit much to hope for, admittedly. "Okay. What about blood magic? Edward uses it in conjunction with his natural magic. Could I do that?"

The smile disappeared. "You already have."

I took a breath, and paused.

"Because I drank vampire blood, you mean?" I asked, to clarify.

"And demon blood."

He meant Zorah's blood, I thought. "Is that why her blood hit me harder than even Rans' did?"

"I would imagine so," Albigard agreed.

I made a mental note to talk to Edward again in the future, assuming I managed to live through the coming days and weeks.

"What about life magic?" I asked.

He frowned. "What about it?"

"Edward said you can do both kinds," I clarified. "I saw you use vines to trap the guards at the gateway when we were trying to get back to Earth. That was life magic, right?"

"It was," he said slowly. "The confluence of the two kinds of magic is unusual among Fae. I've never known of a human who successfully combined the two classes."

I nodded, accepting his words. "Can you teach me to control water the way you did when you were getting the silver out of Leonides' chest? I only know how to freeze it or boil it. Not to control how it moves."

"Perhaps," he said. "Let us return to the house and see."

We trekked back to the depressing structure and reconvened in the kitchen, where Albigard spent the next two hours trying to get me to bend the flow of water dripping from the sink faucet without physically touching it. Unfortunately, where Edward was a natural teacher, the Fae... really wasn't. At least, not with humans.

Nevertheless, I eventually managed to deflect the trickle of water an inch or two, though I ended up heating it to the point of steaming at the same time.

"Intriguing," Albigard said. "Perhaps there is hope for you to further your magical education after all."

"Gee, thanks," I told him.

Grumbling aside—that last, successful attempt *had* felt different. It was the first time I'd really understood what he'd been talking about when it came to using magical fields to manipulate matter, rather than raw emotion. I wondered if I might eventually be able to manipulate earth and stone at a distance in such a way. Or—I blushed a bit despite my best efforts—*fire*.

"Seriously, though," I went on, "I *do* appreciate it. I feel like I've been dumped in the deep end with this stuff, and I never know what bit of knowledge or what new ability might be the thing that makes the difference in getting Jace back."

He looked at me with an expression I couldn't quite parse, though it seemed less cold and distant than his usual demeanor.

"It is unlikely your magical abilities will be able to turn the tide against the Unseelie, adept," he said eventually. "That will take something considerably larger than a single person—even a magical one."

I blinked at him, feeling the hole of hopelessness opening up in my chest again. "You know, you and Zorah are both *horrible* at offering reassurance."

His green gaze didn't falter. "You would prefer lies? You already know I'm incapable of those."

"So I'm told," I said on a sigh. "Look… never mind. Thank you for answering my questions and teaching me something new."

"It helped to pass the time, and cost me nothing," he replied, rather than saying 'you're welcome' like a normal person. "Now, though, it appears the bloodsuckers have returned from their hunt. Perhaps you should procure some of their spoils for yourself, and retire for more rest."

"Right," I said, regarding him closely. "The whole 'drinking vampire blood' thing *really* creeps you out, doesn't it?"

"Yes," he replied simply. "It really does."

EIGHTEEN

I ended up opting for a hit of Rans' blood, rather than drinking Zorah's and spending the night physically reliving every vivid detail of how it had felt when Leonides touched me. Then, perversely, I lay awake for a couple of hours obsessing over the memory anyway. I wondered if he was thinking about it, too, and then berated myself for being so distracted when there were far more important things to worry about.

Eventually, I managed to fall asleep, at which point I dreamt of Jace. I would have given anything for my dreams to be some newly awakened magical ability, feeding information about his whereabouts through my subconscious mind. Sadly, they were just the usual psychological flotsam and jetsam, yielding no useful information beyond the newsflash that I blamed myself for his abduction and feared screwing things up again if we ever managed to find him for a rescue attempt.

The morning found me bleary-eyed and groggy, despite the vampire blood I'd consumed and the fact that this was more sleep than I'd gotten in some time. I showered and dressed; I ate a breakfast I didn't taste. The four of us—once again, sans Albigard—piled into Len's car and repeated the drive to the offices of the *Weekly Oracle*.

I tried to moderate my expectations. After the lackluster results of the previous day, it seemed unlikely that this trip would yield much information of use. I told myself this repeatedly, only for my heart to lurch into a gallop when the redheaded guy, Isaac, met us at the reception desk with all the guileless excitement of a happy Labrador Retriever.

"Oh, good! You're here! We think we got something—come on back!" He gestured enthusiastically for us to follow him.

We did, approaching what I gathered was Derrick's desk. At least, Derrick was currently hunched over it, tapping away single-mindedly at the keyboard with Óliver leaning over his shoulder.

"Go on... show them what you found!" Isaac insisted, and his excited tone had my heart leaping up to lodge in my throat.

We crowded around the blocky cathode-ray monitor as Derrick pulled up what looked like a news article with one hand on the mouse, while reaching for a stack of printouts with the other hand.

"Hey, so, we did find something that seems pretty promising," he said, rifling through the sheets of paper and pulling one out. "There were seventy-three locations that seemed like they might fit the bill—remote, not much in the way of population, and a confluence of ley lines."

Isaac broke in, seemingly unable to contain himself. "Then Óliver decided to cross-reference them with news stories from the past year, to see if anything interesting popped up, right? And he hit pay-dirt late last night."

"Where?" I asked breathlessly.

"And what kind of pay-dirt?" Rans added.

Derrick waved at the news article on the screen. *Bird Flu Outbreak Decimates Easter Island*, I read, in blocky letters. A smaller subtitle lay beneath. *Tourism Suspended Indefinitely – Airport Closed to Commercial Traffic*.

"Easter Island," I echoed blankly. "That's… the place with the giant stone statues of heads, right?"

I was embarrassed to admit that I wouldn't have a clue where to find it on a map. Atlantic? Pacific? I exchanged glances with Zorah, who looked equally mystified.

"That's the one," Derrick agreed. "We almost struck it from the original list, because it has a decent-sized city with an airport and a naval base — not to mention the tourist trade. But in the purest physical sense, you can't get much more remote. The nearest population center is, like, sixteen hundred miles away… and that's just another tiny island with a town of maybe five hundred people on it."

He pulled up a window that looked like Google Maps, only it had a bunch of curved lines superimposed over the continents and oceans.

"Are those ley lines?" I asked, trying to make sense of the confusion on the screen.

"Yep," Derrick agreed. "Look."

He clicked and dragged the map, zooming in on the South Pacific. The continents disappeared off the edges of the screen, leaving open ocean crisscrossed by red lines. He zoomed, and zoomed, and zoomed even more, re-centering on a patch of undifferentiated blue where three of the ley lines crossed. More zooming, and finally a green-and-brown speck became visible. Eventually, it resolved into a roughly triangular island.

"Sixty-three square miles with the population either dead of the flu, or evacuated to better medical facilities," Óliver said, "and the border closed to outside arrivals. There's a city on the southwest coast… abandoned now, or close to it. If I needed to hide a bunch of kids somewhere no one would notice, I can think of worse places to do it."

My breath caught in my lungs. Was Jace trapped on this tiny speck in the South Pacific?

"I agree those are some compelling facts," Leonides said. "But are there any other places that made the cut? It's a big planet."

"Five of the other sites also had some mention of odd phenomena in the past six months," Isaac replied. "But those were for climatological or seismic stuff. Three of them are places where it would be really difficult for humans to stay alive without a serious support team — deserts and mountains. One was in the middle of Lake Tanganyika in Africa — "

"And the last one was in Antarctica, but the permanent research team there has been reporting in regularly," Derrick finished. "The news story related to that one was about record high temperatures, but I expect it's just climate change. Other than that, the scientists stationed there haven't reported anything odd."

"The one on the lake in Africa, though," Zorah said. "It's conceivable they could be keeping the kids on some kind of ship, right? Like a freighter or a cruise liner?"

Rans frowned. "Conceivable, yes."

Leonides looked thoughtful. "If they were going to do that, though... why not choose an ocean, and surround the ship with saltwater rather than freshwater?"

"That's a very salient point," Rans agreed. "Two birds with one stone, and all that."

"There's a hell of a lot of saltwater around Easter Island," Zorah pointed out.

They were talking about demons, I realized. If the Fae wanted to minimize the chance that Nigellus and his buddies would come snooping around, surrounding themselves with saltwater was apparently an effective way to do it.

The *Weekly Oracle* guys were exchanging curious glances.

"So..." Derrick began, "are we talking little green men here? Because—not gonna lie, guys—none of this really sounds like little green men."

Rans smiled a dangerous smile. "Oh, it's far more interesting than that. Gather 'round, mates, and let me tell you a tale."

Three pairs of eyes settled on him avidly, and the vampire's gaze lit with inner light.

"The tale is this—you helped us find the information we needed, and we promised to let you know if we found anything interesting in return. Beyond that, you don't remember the details of the conversation, except that we were *ever* so grateful for your help. The end."

My pendant flared as Rans flexed his power, and I redirected the magic away from me almost without thinking about it. Without a tinfoil hat in sight, however, Derrick, Óliver, and Isaac's expressions grew vacant and faraway.

"Right," Rans said briskly. "We'll be off now."

"Bye, Hypnos," Zorah said. "Good to see you again."

"Thank you for this," I added. "Seriously... *thank you*."

Leonides had nothing to add, and we left the three men staring after us, blank-eyed and slack-jawed. Even though I knew they were perfectly fine and would snap out of it the moment we were gone, I still felt a faint shiver of disquiet run through me.

We returned to the car. Leonides pulled his door shut with a groan of protesting metal. He leaned forward intently in the back seat, elbows on knees.

"We need to get ourselves on firmer footing before we proceed any further with this," he said. "Vonnie, Zorah, and I are pretty much ghosts after the building exploded. No I.D., no money, no nothing. And we can't do any kind of decent research or prep work at the Fae Motel without access to phones or internet."

With a jolt, it struck me that this situation marked the first time I'd seen Leonides utterly without conventional resources—and that was a huge part of what had felt 'off' about him since he'd recovered physically from his injuries. My ex-boss and recurring hot mistake was the guy with the drawer full of burner phones and the collection of offshore bank accounts. He was the one you went to when you needed a fake identity and international plane tickets in twelve hours flat.

Now, he had the clothes on his back and very little else.

"Hmm," Rans mused. "Normally, I'd say we could bring in some tech and keep it in the basement while keeping Albigard on the top floor... or vice versa. But with the entire property warded, that's probably a good way to fry a bunch of circuitry."

"You've still got I.D. and cash, though," Zorah told him. "That's something."

I tried to kick-start my brain. "Could we get a hotel room nearby, and use that as a secondary base of operations for internet research, and whatever other things we need to do by phone or email?"

"That works," Leonides said. "If I can get hold of Gina, I can probably get us some new travel documents in a reasonable amount of time."

If Easter Island was closed to air traffic, I wasn't sure that helped us. It did, however, raise a different question.

I swallowed and wet my lips. "So... do we have any idea what our status actually is, here? I mean, are we presumed dead? Or are the Fae likely to be watching anyone we might try to contact? Rans already talked to Len once..."

Rans tapped a finger on the steering wheel pensively. "There's been no obvious attempt to suppress news stories related to the explosion, though we have no way of knowing if those stories have been, shall we say, *massaged*. As of my last check, your names have been notably absent from any of the reporting. The authorities have recovered four bodies so far, names withheld pending notification of next of kin. An additional five people made it out with varying levels of injury."

Beside me, Leonides' expression might have been carved from stone.

"They're still calling it a search and rescue operation," Rans continued. "Though I expect that will shift to 'recovery' within the next twenty-four hours or so."

"So everything's still up in the air," I summarized. "They won't know for sure if we're buried in the rubble."

"Not unless they have some very un-Fae-like levels of technological surveillance on Len's phone, anyway," Zorah cautioned.

Leonides sighed. "If we're seriously considering a reconnaissance mission to the South Pacific, we can't tackle it like we're the fucking Lone Ranger."

Rans was still tapping his fingers restlessly against the wheel. "I'm not entirely sure that's true."

Leonides glared at him in the rearview mirror. "Yeah, but here's the thing… we established a hell of a long time ago that you're bent in the head."

"No, hear me out, though," Rans insisted. "The main reason for tapping funds and constructing new identities that might be traced is for *travel*, right?"

"Right…" Leonides said slowly.

Zorah gasped. "Oh, I get it! This place is on a confluence of ley lines…"

"… and we have access to a pissed-off faerie who desperately doesn't want the Fae Court to move from Dhuinne to Earth," Rans finished.

Silence settled for a beat.

"You're suggesting we have Albigard zap us onto Easter Island with no prep and no backup," Leonides said flatly. "Yeah… that's a *no* from me."

Rans shot him a dark look through the mirror. "No, Guthrie. I am not suggesting we have Tinkerbell zap us onto Easter Island with no prep and no backup. I am suggesting that leaving a trail—digital or otherwise—which might conceivably be found and followed, is not necessarily helpful or in our best interests at this juncture."

"That still leaves the need for computer access and research," Leonides shot back. "Instead of mesmerizing those kids into forgetting what we talked about, you should have mesmerized them into printing out every relevant scrap of information relating to Easter Island for us as hard copy."

Rans did, in fact, look a bit sheepish at that. "Ah. Yes… well, it's too late now. Fine. Compromise. I'll pick up a couple of laptops from the nearest pawnshop, and spring for a hotel room with Wi-Fi access."

My brows drew together. "Uh… how much cash are you carrying, anyway?"

Rans shrugged. "Only a few thousand dollars, so I fear they won't be very *impressive* laptops."

"Someday I'll get used to how rich people think," I told him.

He shot me a tight grin.

Zorah took pity on me. "You and Guthrie can camp out in a hotel and spend the day learning everything there is to know about Easter Island... particularly about what happened to the people there. Meanwhile, we'll take what we already know and brainstorm with Albigard. We can re-convene tonight and try to put everything together."

I resolutely did not panic over the idea of being stuck alone in a hotel room with Leonides for hours on end. We had more important things to worry about now.

"Okay," I said, without looking at him. "Sounds like more of a plan than we had this time yesterday, anyway."

Inside my chest, my heart beat an unsteady rhythm. *We know where he is, we know where Jace is*, it seemed to chant. But were we right? And even if we were, could three vampires, a Fae, and a human witch successfully storm an island half a world away to get my son back?

NINETEEN

As promised, Rans drove the pimpmobile to the nearest pawn store that dealt in laptops and cell phones. I knew from unfortunate personal experience that many of them didn't—cell phones, especially, were too commonly stolen to make it worth their while. A lot of pawnbrokers didn't want to mess with the potential liability.

The rather unreassuringly named Pawn Qween, however, had no such scruples. Rans disappeared inside the shop and returned fifteen minutes later with two laptops, two cell phones, and an extra charger for the burner phone Leonides had given me, which had miraculously survived having a building fall on it. In the car, Rans activated both of the new phones in his—fake—name, and we all synced contacts.

From there, Zorah found the closest hotel to Albigard's hidden house... which wasn't all that close, to be honest. Now that I had Google Maps open and Rans had given us the location of the safehouse, I could finally start to orient myself a bit. The property was in a place called Homer Glen, backing up to Messenger Woods Nature Preserve. I suppose that explained the overgrown plant life in Albigard's expansive back yard. The hotel was maybe eight miles away from it, off an exit on Interstate 80.

"Um…" I said, eyeing the huge, modern-looking structure as Rans pulled into the lot. "This doesn't look like the kind of place that takes cash and rents rooms by the hour."

"Of course it does," Rans said cheerfully, easing the Lincoln into a parking spot designed for a much narrower vehicle.

He turned off the engine and pulled the key out of the ignition, tossing the keyring over his shoulder without looking, fuzzy dice and all. Leonides snatched it neatly out of the air. A moment later, Rans stretched a hand back, holding a folded mass of bills between his fingers. With a jolt, I realized they were hundreds.

Leonides took it. "You two flying straight back to Albigard's, then?" he asked.

"It's probably easiest," Rans replied. "You can drive back and meet us when you've finished your research. Hopefully we'll have the beginnings of a strategy hashed out by that time."

Zorah let out an indelicate snort. "Or else he and Tink will spend the entire day sniping at each other. One or the other."

Rans raised an eyebrow. "*Excuse* me. We're quite capable of sniping at each other and devising strategy at the same time. In fact, after nearly six hundred years we've practically raised it to an art form."

"God help us all," Leonides muttered. He opened the shrieking backseat door, scooping up the bag holding the two laptops and all of the various chargers—except the one Zorah had taken for her new phone—as he went. I scooted across and followed him out.

Rans and Zorah joined us, locking their doors with the old-fashioned mechanical push-knobs before closing them. I did the same with the back door and slammed it shut, after double-checking that Leonides still had the keys.

Rans turned to me. "Now, Vonnie... do make sure to have him back by, shall we say, nine?" he said. "Otherwise, we'll assume something's gone wrong and come looking."

I rolled my eyes at him, since the alternative would be blushing. "Sure thing, *Dad*. We'll be home in time for curfew."

"See that you are," he retorted mildly. "I understand the necessity of getting out from under the Fae tech-killing cloud, but I'm not really all that sanguine about splitting up in these circumstances."

"There are an extremely limited number of ways anyone could have tracked us here," Leonides reminded us. "Stop fussing, and go make a plan. Preferably one that's not completely suicidal."

"Right," Zorah said. "One minimally suicidal long-distance rescue plan, coming up. Watch your backs, you two."

She gave each of us a quick hug, and it occurred to me that I wasn't the only one who hadn't gotten over what happened in St. Louis quite yet. Leonides lifted an arm to squeeze her shoulders in return, his stony exterior cracking briefly for his granddaughter. Watching them, I contemplated how few people in his life there appeared to be with whom he ever really let his guard down.

Not that I had loads of room to talk on that subject, but things had gotten better for me on the 'friend' front in the short months since I'd become a bartender at the Vixen's Den. Indeed, life in general had become better in some ways… and immeasurably worse in others.

After a final farewell, Rans and Zorah wandered off to find an out-of-the-way corner where no one would notice two people turning into mist and flying away. Which… left me alone in the parking lot with Leonides. He looked at me and sighed.

"We're making progress, Vonnie," he said. "I just want to make sure we don't rush in without a plan and end up getting our asses handed to us."

The drumming, unrelenting maternal need to *act* had been such an integral part of me since that fateful phone call from Richard's mother, that it was basically a second heartbeat at this point.

"I know," I told him softly. "Believe me—I get it."

Right now, my greatest fear was screwing it up somehow… getting my chance to save Jace, and blowing it.

He nodded. "Let's go and get started, in that case."

We entered the shining lobby of the almost-certainly-wouldn't-take-cash hotel. Fortunately, there was only one other customer at the desk, and she left as we were walking up.

I smiled nervously as the desk clerk greeted us. Leonides requested a double without batting an eye, and peeled off a couple of hundred-dollar bills to pay for it.

The clerk's smile grew fixed. "I'm sorry, sir," he said. "Debit or credit only. I'm afraid we don't accept cash."

"Yes, you do," Leonides replied in a monotone. My pendant tingled against my chest.

The receptionist blinked. "Yes... sorry. That will be one hundred thirty-nine dollars, please. If you'll just sign here..." he scooted a printout toward us.

"No," Leonides told him.

The clerk tugged the paper away abruptly. "Of course. Let me just get your key cards."

"Yup. Hardly creepy at all," I murmured, as the harried man went rummaging for our plastic cards.

"Shut up," Leonides said under his breath, looking distinctly uncomfortable.

"Room 327," the desk clerk said, and gave him his change before handing the key cards to us. "Enjoy your stay."

"Will do," I told him. "Um... have a nice day."

The third-floor room was near the end of the hall, close to the ice and vending machines. I bummed ten dollars so I could stock up on enough salty snacks and caffeinated beverages to get me through until dinner. When I entered the room, it was to find Leonides already plugging in the laptops—one at the little corner desk, and one into a receptacle above the bedside table.

It was a nice room; clean and tasteful, not that it really mattered. Though, for a hundred thirty-nine bucks per night, I supposed it would be.

"Dibs on the bed as a workspace," I said. "What are we thinking, here? Maps and general info, plus any information we can find about the supposed flu outbreak?"

"Sounds about right," he agreed. "Don't access any cloud accounts, though I will take a chance by logging into my VPN so we can route our internet searches through Sweden or the Netherlands."

"Are we going to have to write down or memorize everything we need to take back to Albigard and the others?" I asked, thinking—not for the first time—that the Fae technology issue was a complete pain in the ass.

The corner of his mouth ticked down. "I think we're at least going to need printouts of the maps. Both of the island itself, and the nearest islands to it. The hotel has a printer downstairs. It's not completely without risk, but as electronic footprints go, that's a pretty faint one."

I frowned at him. "Didn't the *Weekly Oracle* guys say the nearest island was, like, sixteen hundred miles away?"

"The nearest *inhabited* island," he replied. "I'm hoping there are uninhabited ones considerably closer than that."

Wanting to get started and finished with the task as fast as possible, I piled a bunch of pillows against the headboard, arranged my snacks around me for easy access, and powered up the computer. The good news was, the laptop was clean—fresh off a factory reset. The bad news was, I didn't get too far into the Windows 10 setup process before I was prompted to create or login to a Microsoft account… and there was no option to skip the step.

"Erm…" I began.

"Turn off the Wi-Fi connection and start over," Leonides said without looking up. "Then try to create an account, and the error page that pops up will have a 'skip' button at the bottom. That should allow you to make an offline account."

"Anonymity shouldn't be this complicated," I muttered, doing as he said.

"Tell me about it," he agreed.

I floundered through the process of making an account on the laptop that wasn't connected to anything external, and was eventually rewarded by pristine, dark blue desktop wallpaper with an image of illuminated window panes. At which point, I immediately had to install a bunch of security updates.

Evidently, Leonides was stuck on the same step. "Should've made Rans buy MacBooks instead," he grumbled.

I made an ambiguous noise in response, never having owned a Mac. Rather than focus on the ensuing awkward silence, I tore into a bag of chips and popped open a can of Dr. Pepper. After a bit more than ten minutes, I was finally ready to go.

"Okay, how do I do the VPN thing?" I clicked through the menu. "And, uh, where's Internet Explorer?"

Leonides shot me a strange look from his spot at the desk. "How old was your last laptop, exactly?"

I wrinkled my nose. "Not sure, but it was running Windows 8. Barely."

He shook his head, as if in dismay. "Edge is the default browser now. And it's probably easier for me to set up the VPN than try to explain the steps." He gestured for the laptop.

I scooted off the bed and took it to him, watching over his shoulder as he deftly installed a little icon in the taskbar and logged into his VPN account. The icon lit up green.

"Hopefully the company is as secure as I'm paying them to be," he said. "If the status icon turns red, the connection has been dropped. Oh, and this is Edge." He hovered the cursor over a swoopy green and blue icon.

"Okay, cool. I think I'm set." I took the laptop back from him. "Do you want to take logistics research or influenza outbreak research?"

"Logistics, for choice." He handed me a pad of hotel stationery and a pen for Fae-friendly note taking. "And since I already know you're old-school, here."

"On it." I returned to my comfy nest of pillows and snacks and got settled. After convincing Edge that, no thank you, I didn't wish to set up a customized home page right now, I got down to business—scrounging in my memory for every piece of Google-fu I'd ever picked up over the years.

As had already been established, I knew jack about Easter Island beyond 'the place with big stone statues of heads.' So I started out with a quick perusal of the Wikipedia page about the island and its native inhabitants, the Rapa Nui. From the little I'd learned about ley lines, I guess it wasn't surprising that an island with a confluence of them would also have a populace with such a deep view of spirituality.

It was ironic that—at least as far as modern-day researchers seemed to think—erecting the giant stone monuments dedicated to the spirits of their ancestors had ended up destroying the ecology of the tiny, sixty-three-square-mile island. Apparently, they'd cut down all the large trees to use as rollers for moving the heavy statues from the quarry to the coasts, leaving insufficient wood for boat-building, and thereby reducing their ability to fish.

A bunch of bird species also died out, and the tree loss caused soil erosion that devastated the island's agriculture. The human population subsequently plummeted from more than fifteen thousand people to fewer than three thousand. Then, to top things off, the Europeans arrived, with roughly the sort of results you'd expect. Next came slave raids, and smallpox, and by the time things were finished, there were only a hundred or so people left.

From that point, the native population slowly recovered, and eventually the island became part of Chile. A prominent landowner introduced tourism and archaeological research to the island, after which things stuttered along — with the occasional political hiccup — until the recent spate of news stories hit.

The total population in 2012 had been fifty-seven hundred people, about sixty percent of them native, and forty percent foreign. Hanga Roa, our probable destination, was the only major city — home to all but a tiny fraction of the people on the island. Most of the rest of the place was full of sheep and horses roaming loose. The economy was a mix of agriculture, fishing, government services, and the biggie — tourism.

At least, it had been until about six months ago.

There were a surprising number of articles available, given that today was the first I'd heard about it. However, they were all pretty vague, and rehashed the same few facts, as though there had been a single press release from somewhere, with no real follow-up. Which, I supposed, made sense if it was a Fae plot, or even a Fae hoax.

Supposedly, a previously unknown strain of bird flu had taken root in Hanga Roa, decimating the population over a period of weeks and completely overwhelming the single modern hospital on the island. The Chilean government subsequently evacuated the survivors to Santiago and quarantined them, and a couple of very brief articles from a few weeks later stated that the virus had been contained and there was no evidence of further spread. The island had been closed to outside visitors as a precaution, with only a skeleton staff at the naval base staying on to enforce the travel ban.

Try as I might, I could find no other information—no forum posts from people who'd been there, no personal interviews with survivors... only a handful of posts from would-be vacationers bemoaning the fact that the island was still closed to tourists, months later.

"I have a feeling this is it," I told Leonides. "This is our smoking gun. It's just too convenient otherwise."

I filled him in on what I'd found, and he nodded. "An abandoned city, with enough infrastructure and agriculture to support a small group of Fae and kidnapped children. A few other humans remaining there for security—ones who are already used to taking orders. We know the Fae like to use the police for their own ends. Why not the military?"

I shivered, remembering the SWAT team in the woods in Missouri.

"What about your end of things?" I asked, to distract myself. "Did you find any other islands close by?"

He made a disgruntled noise. "Turns out they weren't kidding about it being isolated. Literally the nearest piece of rock jutting up from the ocean... is two hundred fifty miles away."

"Wow," I said.

"And it's exactly that, too—thirty-seven acres of rock jutting up from the ocean. *Isla Salas y Gómez*, by name. You could practically fit three of it onto that hunting property near Mark Twain Forest."

I tried to picture it, and pulled up some photos on Google when I failed. *Yup*. Rocks. Black ones, set against an aquamarine sea.

"So... we'd be using this place for what, exactly?" I asked.

"Base of operations, and possibly a fallback position," he replied grimly. "Assuming we can even get to it."

Because we weren't taking a plane, or a boat. We were taking... a Fae with an attitude problem.

"Demons would fucking hate that place," Leonides mused.

"Yeah," I agreed. "If they don't like saltwater, I can see why Nigellus shanghaied you into this mess rather than deal with it himself."

He grunted. "Nigellus shanghaied me into this because demons are assholes."

"So are Fae," I pointed out.

"As far as I've been able to tell, all supernaturals are assholes," he grumbled.

"Except Zorah?" I prompted.

"Except Zorah," he agreed.

"And you," I added.

"No, I was including myself, actually," he said. "Right. Let's figure out what we need as hard copy and get this show on the road."

TWENTY

I was surprised to discover that hours had passed while we slid down the research rabbit hole. It was mid-afternoon, and the bed around me was a wasteland of empty, crumpled bags and piled notes.

"I think I've got everything relevant from my end put on paper," I told Leonides.

"Which just leaves a bunch of maps at various scales to print out," he said. "I'll go downstairs and take care of that."

"Hang on," I said, gathering my snack-food detritus and shoving it in the trash. "I might as well come down with you so we can leave right afterward. It's not like there's a lot here to pack up."

There was a different reception clerk on duty when we descended. The little office area with the printer, scanner, and fax machine was already in use, and I shifted restlessly on the balls of my feet as we waited for the person in front of us to be done. Leonides had more to print out than I would have guessed. I folded the resulting pile into the notepad of stationery I'd swiped from the room to keep everything contained.

"Make sure your laptop is powered off and not just asleep," Leonides said, suiting action to word with his computer. "No point in trashing them, even if we may not need them again."

"Already done," I assured him. I was still a bit nebulous on the extent of the Fae effect on technology. I gathered they *could* control it, but doing so took concentrated effort. And apparently the fact that Albigard's place was warded with Fae magic added an additional wrinkle. To be safe, I'd also powered my phone off while packing everything up.

It still felt odd—I could barely remember a time from my childhood when people weren't connected twenty-four seven by phone and 'net, and I said as much to Leonides.

He snorted. "I can. If you'd asked me a week ago, I'd have said I missed it. Turns out, I really don't."

We turned in our key cards at the desk. The female reception clerk's brow furrowed with confusion when she tried to look up our account, only to smooth out when Leonides flashed glowing vampire eyes at her and said, "Don't worry about it."

"Have a lovely day," she told us. "Thanks for staying with us."

We left with our plastic bag full of printouts, handwritten notes, and secondhand electronics. The pimpmobile waited patiently in the parking lot, sticking out like a rusty and bullet-riddled sore thumb. Leonides looked at it and sighed.

"At least it runs," I reminded him. "And it's Fae-proof."

He shook his head ruefully and unlocked the front doors, opening mine for me. I eased inside, setting the bag on the floor by my feet.

"There's an element of cliché around me driving this thing that I don't much appreciate," he muttered, once he'd settled in the driver's seat and adjusted the mirrors.

I couldn't help my huff of amusement. "I'd've driven if you asked me, you know. Besides, without a feathered hat, a fur-trimmed overcoat, and silver-tipped cane, you're missing the complete cliché package."

He shook his head in disgust again before turning the key in the ignition. The engine purred into life. Leonides let it warm up for a minute while he checked the directions on his phone, evidently committing them to memory before he powered it off.

"Let's just say, this isn't how I pictured my week going when I woke up the day before yesterday," he said.

At that, I sobered abruptly. He backed the car out of the parking spot, muttering a bit about its ridiculous size. We exited onto the highway, and after a few minutes, the silence began to feel oppressive.

"What will you do now?" I asked abruptly, the words slipping out against my better judgment.

He shot me a perplexed glance. "Go to Easter Island and try not to get killed, at a guess."

But I shook my head. "No, that's not what I mean." I swallowed to wet my throat. "Your home. It's… gone."

An unpleasant cold sensation lodged in my stomach as I thought about the building that had housed the Vixen's Den and Leonides' penthouse — now little more than a pile of rubble.

He cocked an eyebrow. "The paperwork and insurance is probably going to be a nightmare, especially on Gina's end. But it's not like I lived there my whole life. Far from it. It was just a building."

"You seemed happy there," I said softly.

I watched him frown in profile. "Not… particularly?"

"Settled, then," I tried. "You had roots in that place."

He glanced at me long enough to take in my expression. "A demon tried to kill me in the bedroom of that penthouse apartment. I was turned into a vampire there. Not all roots are good." He seemed to weigh his words for a moment. "Vonnie… I'm a disgustingly rich person, with access to a powerful network comprised of other disgustingly rich people. If you need to worry about something, try worrying about the next few days — not about my next real estate investment."

It might have sounded harsh, but I didn't get the impression he'd intended it that way. When I didn't answer right away, he shot me another quick look.

"What about you?" he asked.

"What about me?" I replied blankly, because as far as I knew, my crappy little apartment was still standing.

"Say we manage not to get killed," he continued patiently. "Say you get your son back, and the world doesn't end in Fae slavery. What will you do?"

I opened my mouth, paused for a couple of seconds, and closed it.

"Do you really think that's likely?" I asked eventually.

He shrugged. "No idea. I don't write the scripts; I just seem to get dragged along as a side character."

You're more than that to me, I thought, but thankfully managed to keep it from slipping out. This conversation was not the prelude to some modern-day fairytale, where Leonides asked me to bring Jace to live in his castle like a happy little supernatural family because we'd had sex in a shower stall. This was a man who took in strays, trying to decide if I could be released into the wild again without immediately starving in the streets.

"Well," I said carefully, "I guess there's always a market for bartenders. Without Ivan hanging over my head, maybe I'll start saving up and go finish my paralegal degree."

In my head, I couldn't actually picture that life. It was too normal. Too pat. It made too many assumptions about how the next few days would go. And for some utterly inexplicable reason, it made me feel sort of... *empty*.

We'd left the highway and turned onto a tree-lined road while we'd been talking. Leonides slowed the car as we rounded a bend.

"That's the place, isn't it?" he asked.

I looked at the winding drive disappearing up a hill and into the trees.

"Since it was invisible when I saw it before, I'm not much help," I said, almost relieved at the interruption to my unhappy thoughts.

He turned into the driveway, and once he did, I recognized it from when we'd left for the newspaper offices with Rans driving. The sprawling house lay at the top of the drive, obscured from the road by trees, and Leonides parked the pimpmobile in front of it. The front door was unlocked, somewhat to my surprise—though I supposed since the owner could enter by magic portal, and the place was invisible to everyone else, locks would be a bit redundant.

"Back so soon?" Rans said, poking his head in as we entered the kitchen.

Something in his tone made me wonder if he'd expected us to fall into a hotel bed together the instant we were left alone. I couldn't help scowling at him.

"We got what we needed," I said, a bit brusquely. "The clock's ticking; there wasn't any reason to stick around."

"And quite right, too," he agreed easily. "Our little cut-price council of war is convening in the upstairs living room. Bring whatever you need and come along."

I grabbed a bottle of water from the fridge and dropped the bag containing the computers on the table, fishing out the bundle of papers and trotting up the stairs after the two vampires. Someone had dragged enough chairs into the empty space to accommodate all of us, along with a chipped table scrounged from who-knew-where. An old-fashioned desktop globe sat in the center.

Zorah and Albigard looked up as we approached.

"Hi. So… we have an idea," Zorah greeted. "It's, um, a work in progress, let's say."

"And by that," Rans added, "she means you're probably going to burst an aneurysm when you hear it, Guthrie. Sit down, both of you."

"Wonderful," Leonides said flatly, and gestured me to sit first.

I did, and set the pile of paper on the table in front of me. It felt oddly like preparing for a board meeting back in my MMHA volunteer days.

"So," Zorah began, "we're working on the assumption that we've got an island full of Unseelie Fae holding a group of maybe a couple hundred human children."

My heart jolted. "That many?"

Rans steepled his fingers together beneath his chin. "That's a rough estimate based on information from Nigellus. It's not one hundred percent reliable, simply because more than a thousand children disappear every day in the normal course of things. Untangling the number of children taken by the Fae from garden-variety human kidnapping and runaways is an inexact science, to put it mildly."

"At any rate, we expect to find a big group of children being held by a somewhat smaller group of Fae," Zorah continued.

"There may be controlled human military involved, too," Leonides interrupted. "Chile maintains a naval base there. But we can get into those details later."

Zorah nodded. "Makes sense. Okay, so we need to get into a Fae-controlled area. Fortunately, we've got our own Fae."

Albigard shot her a flat look, presumably at her use of the possessive language.

I frowned. "I hate to say it, but I don't get the impression Albigard is all that popular with the rest of the Unseelie these days."

"He's not," Zorah agreed. "But it won't matter, because magical glamour is a particular skill of his."

I blinked at her. "Um, how should I put this? My experience of magic has *not* been very glamorous to date."

She let out a snort of laughter. "Different kind of glamour, babe. I'm talking about magically changing your appearance… or someone else's."

I remembered Edward mentioning something about that. He hadn't gone into much detail, since it wasn't the sort of thing I was likely to be able to do—no matter how much vampire blood I drank.

"Oh. Okay." I looked at Albigard. "So you could pretend to be a different Fae? One without a bunch of wanted posters tacked up all over Dhuinne?" I paused. "Hang on. Isn't that basically like lying?"

He looked at me like a parent might look at a toddler asking annoying questions. "Perhaps it would be, if I actually claimed to be the person in question. Which I will not be doing, obviously."

I looked at him like a not-crazy person might look at a crazy person.

Zorah huffed out a breath. "Yeah, don't bother, Von. It's a whole thing. And there's something to be said for letting people make their own assumptions, I guess."

"Can we fast forward to the part I'm not going to like?" Leonides said.

Rans took over the thread. "In addition to glamouring himself, Alby will also glamour Vonnie to look like a teenager."

Zorah butted back in. "And since she has magic, it will be plausible that he's dropping off another kidnapped girl for the Fae's collection. At which point both of them will have access to the *other* kids—including, hopefully, Jace."

"No," Leonides said immediately.

But my heart was already pounding with sudden excitement at the beautiful simplicity of the idea. "Yes. I'll do it."

Leonides' hard gaze landed on me. "No. You won't. That's a horrible plan."

I stood up abruptly, my chair legs catching and dragging on the carpet. "Look. I told you from the beginning that nothing mattered except getting Jace back," I snapped. "You may be able to bend human minds, but you do *not* get to tell me when and how I go to him, now that we finally have a chance."

Air swirled around me, and I realized with a jolt that my emotions were escaping as magic—the control that had become largely second nature to me threatening once more to burst its banks.

"It's dangerous to stand between a female and her offspring, vampire," Albigard drawled.

"Listen to the pretty boy," I counseled past a clenched jaw. "He's talking sense."

Leonides didn't back down. "So you get to your son. At which point, you're trapped with him. How does that help the situation?"

In my peripheral vision, I saw Albigard wave an airy hand. "You think I will not choose a guise that gives me unquestioned access to the facility? While the adept locates her son, I will perform reconnaissance among the other Fae. When I have the information I need, I will inspect the human children, and portal the three of us away to safety."

"Sounds good," I said without missing a beat. "Like I said—I'm in. When can we go?"

"Yeah, we kind of need to go over whatever information you two were able to come up with first," Zorah said gently. "Maybe sit down again, babe?"

But I was still glaring at Leonides, and nothing in Leonides' expression said he was ready to back down.

"This is insane," he said, "and it's not happening. You want to pop down to the South Pacific and let the people who can transform into mist do reconnaissance? Fine. Albigard wants to play spy? *Fine*. But what the hell do you think is going to happen when you slip up and the Fae find out who you are?"

"Why the hell do *you* assume I'm going to slip up?" I shot back angrily.

"Enough." Rans' voice was quiet, but the power behind it rolled through the room. His blue eyes landed on Leonides, and they held a coldness I'd never seen in them before. Leonides stiffened beneath the weight of that heavy gaze.

"I warn you, Rans," he said through gritted teeth. "Don't even *try* to pull this kind of vampire pecking order shit on me right now."

"I wouldn't normally," Rans replied in an even tone, "but this isn't just about a mother going after her missing son. It's about a powerful race on the brink of taking over the planet and crushing humanity beneath their boot heel. Albigard needs a reason to be on Easter Island, and Vonnie is the only magical human to whom we currently have access. If the plan also gives her a chance to rescue Jace, so much the better."

The tendons in Leonides' neck stood out as he strained beneath his sire's seven-hundred-year-old power.

"Rans," he managed, "I swear to god, you are *this* close to putting a bullet in our friendship."

"*Stop.*" I slammed my palms down, the globe rattling. The pile of papers in front of me fanned out as the table shook. "*Listen* to me, damn it. In what world is this your decision, Leonides? Jace is *my* son. This is *my* risk to take, or not to take. And in case it's not clear, *I'm fucking taking it*. You get to decide whether you're going to help, or whether you're going to flip us the middle finger and go buy another nightclub to play with. *That's it*. That's the only decision you get right now."

TWENTY-ONE

The silence that fell in the wake of my words was so complete that my ears rang for a few seconds... or maybe it was just the rush of blood from my pounding heart. "*Damn*, girl," Zorah said eventually. She shifted her gaze to Leonides. "So, Guthrie, what's it going to be? Because she's right on all counts."

Rans' power eased, the effect similar to a great bird of prey furling its wings. "Indeed. What is your answer, Guthrie? Because I'm sorry, old friend, but this will be happening, with or without you. Personally, I would much prefer it to be *with*."

Leonides looked frozen, his gaze flickering between Rans and Albigard. "If either of you end up getting her killed, you'll have things to worry about besides the Fae."

Rans continued to watch him closely. "While I completely understand the sentiment, that's not really an answer."

Exasperation bloomed in Leonides' expression, as well as in his voice. "What the fuck do you *think* the answer is? You seriously believe I'm going to run back to St. Louis and sit on my ass while the Fae take over the world?"

Relief flooded my chest. Zorah, who'd been watching the exchange with wide brown eyes, relaxed. Rans didn't—not completely.

"And the plan?" he prompted.

Leonides' jaw worked. "It's not a plan. It's Russian goddamned roulette, with the barrel pointed at Vonnie's head."

He still wanted to stop me.

"Look me in the eye," I told him, hearing the steel in my own voice. "Leonides, look me in the eye *right now*, and tell me you're going to try to keep me from getting to Jace."

He met my gaze, frustration leaping from his eyes as visibly as the violet swirls of vampiric inner light. I didn't blink. Neither did he.

"They're not going to let me stop you," he said, when the silence grew unbearable. "But if you're in imminent danger and I can do something about it, I fucking *will*."

I didn't look away. "And if you decide to do something that stops me from saving Jace, I will never speak to you again."

His expression might as well have been carved from agate. "As long as you're still alive to give me the silent treatment, I'll learn to live with it."

I supposed there was something to be said for knowing where you stood with a person. Though right now, I wasn't sure what it was.

Albigard cleared his throat, breaking our uncomfortable staring contest. "If we've quite finished with the tedious mating rituals, could we perhaps discuss the details of this island and its surroundings?"

I exhaled sharply and sat down, finally breaking eye contact—mostly because I suspected we'd be here all day if I waited for Leonides to back down first.

"Yeah," I said. "Of course. We've got maps, along with everything we could track down pertaining to recent events there. What do you want first?"

"The recent events," Albigard suggested. "Your demeanor suggests you are now confident this location is the correct one."

"Pretty confident," I agreed, and ran through the story of the supposed flu virus for him.

He nodded when I was finished. "Plausible. It would not be the first time the Fae have used such a tactic on Earth. Now, the maps?"

I pawed through the messy collection of papers for something that showed Easter Island's general location in the Pacific, and organized others showing different levels of scale while he examined it. Albigard reached a long arm across the table and hooked the globe closer, turning it on its axis to pinpoint the tiny island. I wondered what the point was of doing so, since the printed maps were far more detailed.

A moment later, he rested his fingertips on the globe's surface, a look of concentration crossing his features. My pendant tingled, a wave of gooseflesh prickling up my arms. A confused tangle of glowing lines flared over the globe's textured surface, startling me enough that I jerked backward in my chair.

"What... *is* that?" I asked, thoroughly taken aback.

"A travel-globe," said the Fae, his attention remaining firmly fixed on the spherical model in front of him.

"Those are ley lines, I take it?" Zorah asked.

"Obviously," Albigard replied.

As I watched, he began to pluck the glowing lines like a musician playing an instrument. More and more of them disappeared, until finally, only a handful remained. I rose from my chair so I could look over his shoulder at the blue expanse of the Pacific, crisscrossed by the irregular ridges of tectonic plates.

Four glowing lines converged on a spot roughly one-third of the distance between South America and Australia.

"I thought the guys at the newspaper said there were only three ley lines converging on Easter Island," I said.

Albigard's reply sounded distracted. "The day humans can read the ley lines properly is the day rats stand up on their hind legs and demand citizenship."

"*Nice,*" Zorah observed tartly.

I set another map printout in front of him. "This is the closest land to Easter Island. It's not much—just rocks—but Leonides thinks it might be useful as a fallback position."

"How far away?" Rans asked.

"Two hundred fifty miles, give or take," Leonides said, rejoining the conversation grudgingly.

"Hmm," Rans replied. "Not exactly ideal."

"The island will have been chosen for its inaccessibility," Albigard said. "That's rather the point."

"Can we even get to the other one?" I asked him. "Is it on a ley line, and if not, can you make a portal leading to it?"

"I cannot form a portal to a place I've never been." The Fae held the printout up to the globe, looking between the two. "These two places are part of the same volcanic ridge. The east-west ley line follows the magnetic disturbance caused by a tectonic plate sliding over a hotter area in the planet's mantle. Are there any manmade objects on this islet?"

"There's a navigational beacon," Leonides said, still in a monotone. "It's on the southern tip."

Albigard nodded. "While difficult, I should be able to navigate us to it."

"And more importantly, once you've been there, you can cast a portal to get back to it," Rans said. "That could be useful. Is it likely the Unseelie will have taken any precautions regarding this little pile of rocks?"

The Fae shook his head. "I doubt it. There's nothing of interest there, and two hundred fifty miles is a significant distance. While they have gone some way toward discouraging the approach of either demons or humans, they will not be expecting infiltration by one of their own."

Rans leaned back in his chair and crossed his arms. "So, we're looking at traveling by ley line to the islet — does it have a name, by the way?"

"Salas y Gómez," I told him.

"And from there," he continued, "by ley line to Hanga Roa on Easter Island."

"You and the demonkin should remain on the islet in case things go wrong and backup is needed," Albigard said. "The adept and I will go in under glamour, and Leonides will watch from above as mist. In that way, we will have two options for returning to the islet for assistance. I can cast a portal, and if necessary, a vampire could cover the distance by flying."

I debated insisting that Leonides stay behind and one of the others come with us, but decided it would probably be a waste of effort.

"So you can really make me look like a child?" I asked instead. "Will that mess up the warding on my pendant?"

If the Fae could either see or sense my pendant, it might blow my cover, depending on whether I'd made it onto any Fae 'most wanted' lists after our little escapade in Dhuinne.

"I will endeavor to work around it—easier, since I was present when the warding was crafted."

"Good." I would have left the necklace behind if I had to, but since it was my best defense against Fae mental influence, I'd be much happier having it with me.

Rans met Albigard's eyes and held them. "We are, as you're well aware, relying heavily on your part in this—especially when it comes to what we'll actually find in Hanga Roa. Not to put too fine a point on it, you're the only one with a realistic chance of getting inside the Unseelie's operation there."

Albigard arched a brow. "What's the matter, bloodsucker? Do you doubt my dedication to preventing my people from forsaking the home that created them in favor of this pale imitation?"

"No," Rans said steadily. "Hence our presence around this table. Are you content with the plan as outlined?"

"I am."

"Everyone else?" Rans asked.

Zorah and I nodded. Leonides looked like he was biting his own tongue, possibly while his fangs were extended.

"Very well," Rans said. "What do you need for the glamour, Alby?"

"Time and privacy."

"Then you can have both in the morning," Leonides said. "This is going to be physically and emotionally grueling, and most of us have been running on barely any sleep since St. Louis."

Rans nodded. "Fair enough. You good with that, Albigard?"

"That is acceptable," said the Fae.

"Fine," I agreed, knowing intellectually that it was a reasonable stipulation. Whether I'd actually be able to sleep was a different question entirely.

On a scale of 'one' to 'screwed up,' the fact that all I could think about as I lay tossing and turning in my borrowed bed was how it had felt to sleep in Leonides' arms was... pretty screwed up. I had a vague suspicion that my mind was tossing up those images as a distraction from the knowledge that we were finally going after Jace. Because once I started down *that* path, I would be up all night — no question about it.

Sure enough, when I finally dropped off to sleep due to the cumulative effects of stress and exhaustion, my next awareness was of jolting upright in the bed with a hoarse cry on my lips. Disoriented, I cast around for a light, but the bedside table wasn't where it was supposed to be.

A trickle of memory began to slide in, and I sat blinking in Albigard's guest room, trying to remember if there was a lamp in here, or just the overhead light. After a few seconds, my eyes adjusted, just as a soft knock sounded against the closed door. It wasn't the kind of knock I could picture Leonides using — or Rans or Albigard, for that matter. Which left —

"Zorah?" I croaked.

The door opened, admitting a wedge-shaped slice of illumination from the hallway.

"Yeah, it's me," she said, her shadow cutting through the patch of light as she entered. "You okay?"

I scrubbed at my face. "Nightmare. Par for the course these days."

She didn't ask me if I wanted to talk about it, for which I was grateful. Disjointed wisps of imagery played across my mind's eye, already fading into confusion. Jace. The building explosion. A horribly burned body. Everything muddled together into a toxic stew of fear and failure. I made a concerted effort to shove all of it aside.

"It'll be dawn in an hour or so," Zorah said. "Probably not worth going back to sleep unless you're desperate for it."

"God, no," I replied, swinging my legs out from beneath the covers. "Is Albigard up?"

"Outside, I think," she said. "Communing with the trees, or whatever Fae do in the morning instead of yoga and coffee."

"Good," I grunted. "I'll get myself together, and go find him so we can get started."

She nodded. "Don't forget to eat something first." A pause. "Are you ready for this, Vonnie? Like, *really* ready?"

"Zorah," I told her seriously, "I've been ready for this since about five minutes after I got the phone call he was missing."

"Okay," she said. "Just making sure that you know you can back out—no matter what Rans says."

"Not happening." I rose and stretched, hearing joints pop and crackle. "But I *will* take some vampire blood with that breakfast."

"I'll tell Rans." She hesitated. "Unless you want mine instead?"

I thought about it for a moment. "Probably his, under the circumstances. Fewer distractions. Thanks, though."

I wasn't in a hurry to feel any more conflicted about Leonides than I already did. My libido had no place in what was coming over the next twenty-four hours.

A question I'd been wondering about since last night percolated to the surface of my thoughts.

"How come you're okay with this? You were ready to tear me a new orifice after Leonides and I snuck off to Dhuinne."

Zorah sighed. "Two reasons. First—you *snuck off*. This time, we have something approaching a plan in place, and Rans and I will be there as backup."

"And second?" I prompted.

"We didn't know the world was about to end at the time."

"Makes sense, I guess," I allowed. "Okay... I'd better get ready, so we can get this show on the road. Or, y'know, on the ley line."

Zorah left me to it, so I showered and dressed, went downstairs for nourishment of both the solid and liquid variety, and went outside to find Albigard in the misty predawn.

He was waiting for me at the same flat rock where we'd discussed magic.

"Are you ready?" he asked, echoing Zorah's question.

"Yes," I said simply.

He nodded and rose from his seat on the rock. "Very well. The glamour will be illusion only, though a deep one when viewed from the outside. I will craft an appearance similar to your current skin tone and hair color, and aged past puberty so that your normal way of moving and holding yourself will not appear unnatural."

I nodded. "Jace is fourteen, so that shouldn't be a problem. They're obviously taking kids that old."

"Indeed," he agreed. "Magic among humans has nearly died out over the millennia — as the Fae intended, at least until recently. There are not so many children possessing it that the Unseelie can afford to be picky."

"Okay. Let's do this," I told him. "What do you need me to do?"

"Control your magic so it does not fight mine. That is all." He placed his fingers on my forehead.

I took a deep breath and let it out, picturing my magic sinking inside me, out of his way. Albigard murmured words I felt I should be able to understand, but couldn't. A faint glow wound around my body. I watched as it grew stronger; bending my neck to look at the way it curled around my pendant, avoiding the garnet in its gold setting.

After a few moments of this, the light flared and sank beneath my skin. I felt the magical shift, focusing hard on not letting my own powers react.

"Did it work?" I asked, breathless.

The gray light of dawn was just beginning to filter through the trees. I lifted my arm, spreading my fingers to examine myself. An odd sort of double vision filtered through my senses — an arm that was spindly from rapid teenage growth, the knuckles less lined, and the fingernails showing the smooth glow of youth. Superimposed, I could sense my own familiar arm and hand, but I had to look with my magic, not merely my eyesight.

Albigard gave me a critical once-over. "It will suffice. As, with luck, should this."

My attention moved back to him as he ran a hand down his body, once again mumbling in that unfamiliar language. His appearance shifted before my eyes—his broad shoulders pulling in as though with age. Bleached white-blond hair darkened to an ashy color shot through with streaks of gray. Features that were proud but finely drawn hardened into hard, rugged lines.

An oddly familiar sneer twisted his lips, and I gasped.

"Wait—is that... are you..." I blinked a couple of times. "What was his name? Oren, wasn't it? The asshole from the *Unseelie Court*?"

TWENTY-TWO

Normally, Albigard radiated the kind of haughtiness common to cats—as though he considered you hopelessly tiresome and would probably claw you if you lifted a hand toward him... but maybe in the right mood and under the right circumstances, he would deign to have his chin scratched.

The face looking at me now held a different kind of haughtiness—the haughtiness of a serial killer who considered you prey at best, and at worst, a worthless inanimate object to be used for his own amusement and discarded. I shivered.

"So, you've met him, then," Albigard said in Oren's cold, disdainful voice.

"When you said you'd choose a face that would give you unfettered access, I'll admit this wasn't what I pictured," I told him. "But, hey—if it works..."

"In truth, it pleases me to picture word spreading among the Fae of Oren's visit causing chaos in its wake." This, in his normal, measured tones. "Petty of me, perhaps, but I cannot regret it."

"Was he the one who ordered your sentence?" I asked quietly, remembering thorns piercing flesh... iron constraining magic.

"Indeed," Albigard said. "Which is not to say there was significant opposition to the idea. However, Oren did appear to take a certain... glee... in conveying the Court's ruling."

I was starting to get the impression that Albigard had reached full-on *don't-give-a-fuck* territory when it came to the rest of his race, and I wasn't entirely sure whether that would turn out to be a good thing or a bad thing for us under the circumstances.

"Come," he said. "Let us return and see if the others are ready to leave."

I nodded wordlessly and walked back to the house with him. The vampires had congregated in the kitchen, and all eyes landed on me as I entered.

"*Whoa,*" Zorah said.

Leonides' gaze was piercing, as though he couldn't quite believe what he was really seeing. "Is that... really you?"

I nodded, thinking I should probably find a mirror so I could see the full effect. "More of the David Copperfield shit, right?"

Rans' attention had already wandered past me to take in Albigard's new guise. "Hmm. That's certainly a... bold choice, Alby. Are you going to be able to carry that off?"

I saw Leonides make the mental connection, and blink. Zorah's eyebrows went up.

Albigard sneered Oren's sneer with Oren's face. "Do I look like I have any interest in the opinions of parasites?" The words dripped with Oren's disdain.

Zorah shrugged. "Okay. I'm sold."

"Agreed," Rans said. "Objection withdrawn."

"Does that mean we're ready to go?" I asked. As the time to act grew ever nearer, the seething reservoir of maternal impatience I'd been holding back for weeks felt like it was threatening to burst.

"What's the time zone difference for Easter Island?" Zorah asked.

I sagged a bit, realizing it was probably significant. Similar to Hawaii, maybe?

"Crap, is it still the middle of the night there?" I said. Would we have to wait hours yet? I'd go nuts...

Albigard sighed. "Not at all. One wonders what they teach you humans in school these days. Easter Island is at roughly the same longitude as the western border of Colorado."

I peered at him. "Hang on. It's in the South Pacific. That... can't be right?" A glance at Zorah showed her to be equally perplexed, so at least I wasn't alone.

"Check your maps," Albigard said, the words sounding doubly cutting when delivered in Oren's voice.

"It's nominally in the same time zone we are, thanks to how the lines of demarcation are drawn in the Pacific," Leonides confirmed. "But due to the way daylight savings time works in the southern hemisphere, they're an hour behind us right now."

"More importantly," Rans put in, "In real terms, sunrise for them should be in about fifteen minutes. And believe me when I say, you don't want to land on a tiny, windblown rock in the middle of the ocean until it's light out."

"He's not kidding," Zorah said. "Travel by ley line is… shall we say, *intense*."

"Okay," I allowed. "Fifteen minutes, then." I turned to Albigard. "Do I need to bring anything along?"

Not that I currently had all that much in the way of personal possessions.

"The children are doubtless delivered with only the clothes on their backs, to maximize their sense of disorientation and make them easier to control," said the Fae.

My stomach curled unpleasantly, thinking of Jace being plucked from the airplane, torn away from everything familiar in an instant.

"Right," I said faintly. "I'll just go look in a mirror, then. Back shortly."

I went to the nearest bathroom, trying to come to terms with the next steps I would need to take. So much of it would depend on what we found when we arrived. Were the children being kept in cells? Individually guarded? Or would there be common areas where they could congregate freely?

In reality, Leonides had plenty of cause to be worried about this plan, and I knew it. I just couldn't let it stop us. The world was at stake. My son was at stake. I couldn't fail. I *wouldn't*.

I stepped up to the mirror and stared into it. At some point, someone had taken a damp towel to it and removed most of the dust, though the glass was still streaky.

A wide-eyed teenage girl stared back at me. Still red-haired. Still green-eyed and freckled, like me. Her body held the gawkiness of a youthful

growth spurt. It wasn't me-as-a-teenager, though…
not exactly. I lifted a hand to my pendant—
invisible in the mirror. The girl did the same.

My clothing fit her—the same simple t-shirt
and dark jeans I'd thrown on after my shower this
morning. I wondered how that part worked,
though of course the answer was *magic*.

I'd spent a lot of time thinking about what
would happen once I found Jace. He wouldn't recognize me; the girl in the mirror didn't look like a
photo from my high school yearbook. To him, she
would be a stranger. I would have to be very careful to remember that. Under the circumstances, I
figured my best bet was to appeal to Jace as a fel-
low magical kidnap victim—one with a way out.

I just needed to get to him, or at a minimum,
find out where he was being held in Hanga Roa. If
necessary, Albigard could demand I be taken out of
my cell, at which point he could take me to Jace, as
long as I could tell him where to go. We were banking on Albigard's assumed identity giving him a
level of automatic deference from the other Fae. I
just had to bide my time while he got the information he needed, and then we'd portal away to
freedom.

The clock was ticking. I tore my eyes away
from the stranger in the mirror and returned to the
others in the kitchen. They were loading a collection of items into backpacks—bottled water, food, a
first aid kit. And bagged blood. For the first time, a
skitter of nervousness trickled down my spine.
They were prepping for the aftermath of a battle.

Someone had certainly been busy while I was asleep last night. There were guns on the table, too. And I'd have bet money that the bullets in the pre-loaded clips were iron. With an abrupt jolt, I realized that my mental picture of a stealthy in-and-out job might be the goal of the operation, but it was far from a guaranteed outcome. Worse, if things went to hell, there would be other people in the crosshairs — not just me.

The truly terrible part was, I couldn't let any of it sway me.

I squared my shoulders. "Albigard — I'll try to find Jace and stick with him, assuming the children have any kind of freedom to mingle with each other. But if they don't... if they're kept separated, I may need you to pull rank and, I dunno, demand an inspection of all the kids individually or something."

"Given the goal of the operation, I would expect that the children are controlled on a mental level, rather than a physical one," said the Fae. "You will, of course, need to feign compliance with the Unseelie. They will not be able to see or sense your pendant. Therefore, they will assume that they have power over you. Don't disabuse them of that notion unless you wish to be discovered. Oh, and don't accept gifts of food, drink, or trinkets, obviously. Though the tap water should be safe, and food that you harvest yourself. That is a gift from the island and the humans who lived there; not the Fae."

I took a deep breath and nodded. "Got it." A final, unpleasant thought occurred to me. "Er... has someone told Len what's going on? Or, y'know, anyone else?"

"Len's not in a position to do anything if things go bad," Leonides said. "I got in touch with Gina last night and sent her a file of everything we know, along with Nigellus' contact information so she can pass it on to him if need be. She'll also replace Len's car if it comes to that. It's not like someone can swing by to pick it up and drive it back to him in St. Louis... not with the property warded."

Okay... the others really *had* been busy last night.

"Replace the *pimpmobile*?" I joked weakly. "Are you kidding? Where's Gina supposed to find another 1978 Continental with chrome wheels and bullet holes? One that still runs, I mean."

It fell flat, and it probably deserved to.

"Question for you before we do this, Albigard," Leonides said. "Are you completely recovered? Because I don't want you pulling power from Vonnie — or Zorah, for that matter."

I scowled. "Ignore that. If you need to pull power, then pull it."

And if it comes down to getting Jace out or getting me out, take Jace, I almost added before stopping myself at the last moment. Saying it aloud would only start a fresh round of arguments that I didn't have time for. Albigard, at least, seemed to understand the bond between a mother and her child. He also wasn't driven by sentiment like the others were. Hopefully he would already know to save Jace if he couldn't save me.

"I am recovered," said the Fae, not addressing the rest of it. *Smart man.*

"It's been more than fifteen minutes," I said. "Are we ready?"

"Not remotely," Leonides said, even as he stowed a semiautomatic pistol under each arm in crisscrossing shoulder holsters.

"Yes, we're ready," Rans said, doing the same. He also, I noted, had what looked like a pair of swords strapped to his back. Zorah was arming herself as well—with a pistol and daggers. The vampires, it appeared, were not fucking around. I wasn't sure if that made me feel better or worse.

Zorah and Rans hefted the pair of backpacks, and then Rans turned to Albigard. "Let's go."

Albigard, still in his glamoured guise as Oren, drew a flaming portal in the air of the kitchen. He gestured us through, and I braced myself as the world shifted around me in a dizzying whirl. I stepped out onto a large, overgrown parking lot, nature aggressively reclaiming the ruined patchwork of concrete.

I moved out of the others' way and turned slowly on the spot, my attention caught by a large, square-cornered institutional building that was halfway to being a complete ruin. It looked seventy or eighty years old, at least, and could have been a hospital, or maybe an asylum. The windows were long gone, leaving dark, gaping holes in the structure. Rusty streaks ran down the exterior walls, where acid rain had stained the facade.

When all five of us stood in front of the abandoned building, Albigard gestured behind him and the portal collapsed on itself, disappearing into nothing.

"This is certainly a slice of déjà vu I could've lived without," Zorah muttered. She caught my confused look. "I've been here before. Not a great memory. Don't ask."

"Indeed," Rans agreed grimly. "Alby? I assume the ley line is nearby?"

"Inside," said the Fae, and led the way toward what had once been the main entrance.

Light from the missing east-facing windows illuminated a scene of abandonment and decay. Albigard seemed to know exactly where he was going, though — taking us deeper into the building's skeleton until we reached a stairwell. He, Rans, and Zorah jogged down it without hesitation, but my feet dragged as my brain helpfully tossed up another flashback to the explosion in St. Louis, when Zorah and I had been trapped on the stairs.

A hand closed around my upper arm, and Leonides was in front of me, his expression serious.

"Last chance to rethink this," he said.

I held his dark gaze. "Not happening. Don't ask me again."

His eyes closed for a moment. He opened them and nodded. "I... Vonnie. I give you my word that I'll do everything in my power to get both you and Jace out safely."

Something kicked hard inside my chest, turning the breath I tried to take into a choked noise — one that sounded suspiciously close to a stifled sob. I swallowed hard. Once... twice.

"Thank you." The words were a hoarse whisper.

I closed my hand around his arm as well, mirroring his grip on me. And then... somehow... his lips were covering mine. My eyes squeezed shut, but the press of lips was almost chaste. He pulled away after only a moment.

"Let's catch up to the others now," he said, a bit of hoarseness evident in his voice as well. "Because the next time I do that, I'd really prefer you not to look like a teenager."

A choked breath of laughter ambushed me, despite our grim circumstances. "Right. Yeah, kind of creepy otherwise, I guess... *Mr. Centenarian*."

"You're not helping," he said. "Come on — let's go."

We followed in the others' wake, descending into a moldering basement. The place stank of earth and damp, but fortunately there was a hint of illumination creeping in from high windows that must have been just above ground level. Albigard, Zorah, and Rans were waiting for us near an illuminated patch of bare dirt, where the concrete had been removed in ragged chunks.

"If you're *quite* ready?" the Fae asked, sarcasm dripping from Oren's voice.

"Ready," I said a bit sheepishly, still reeling from that brief press of lips. It bothered me that I couldn't even blame Zorah's succubus blood this time.

"Stand on the dirt," Albigard ordered. "This will be more than usually disorientating, since it will require navigating multiple ley lines. The foot-ing on the other end will doubtless be uneven."

That last part had probably been for my bene-fit, since I'd never seen a vampire look anything less than graceful. Leonides took my upper arm again, and I didn't protest. In fact, I noticed Rans wrapping an arm around Zorah's shoulders as well.

Albigard crouched, placing one hand flat on the damp earth. He spoke the language I couldn't quite understand again, and a faint glow spread outward from the contact until it surrounded all of us. Chicago slipped away.

TWENTY-THREE

Travel by ley lines was like travel by portal, only on steroids. It lasted a lot longer, too. At least… I thought it did. In some ways, it felt like no time at all was passing. Yet it also seemed interminable, according to my scrambled human brain, which obviously wasn't equipped for this kind of shit.

Leonides' firm grip on my arm was the only anchor to reality I had. It was also the thing that kept me from face-planting onto jagged rocks when a flash of light disgorged us on Isla Salas y Gómez.

I'll admit it—I screamed as we stumbled back into existence, the sound emerging sharp and girly. Call it part of my 'teenager' disguise. At least, that was my story and I was sticking to it.

I'd had a sort of mental picture of what it would be like to arrive here. This… wasn't it. Even though the sky was clear and it didn't appear to be stormy, wind and waves battered the pile of dark volcanic rocks… and the five of us now clinging to them. The salt spray was constant and unavoidable. With every wave, seawater poured through and over cracks in the narrow isthmus connecting the two linked peaks that made up the islet.

It was terrifying.

We'd been deposited on the tallest part of the islet, maybe thirty feet above the crashing cauldron of waves below. The navigational beacon stood only a few yards away from us, flashing its blinding white light at regular intervals. Even here, it seemed, humans were drawn to place manmade structures on the ley lines.

Leonides helped me find my footing on a flat-ish section of rock, made dangerously slick by the sea spray.

"Okay," I called, having to raise my voice to be heard above the crashing waves. "This sucks! Whose idea was this again?"

I glared pointedly at Leonides, who looked grim-faced but not remorseful. Meanwhile, Rans had already started scouting out the lee of the jutting rocks, where a ledge with a shallow overhang appeared to offer some protection from the wind.

"This is the closest we'll find to shelter, so Zorah and I will camp here and wait for you to return," he shouted up to us. "If we don't hear back in forty-eight hours, we'll fly across and try to determine what's happening."

I cupped my hands around my mouth and yelled, "How fast can you fly two hundred and fifty miles?"

He and Zorah exchanged a glance. "Two to three hours, at a guess," Rans called back. "Faster with the prevailing winds behind us; slower flying against them."

It was less time than I would have guessed, but it would still be of limited use in a real emergency—especially if Leonides had to fly here from Easter Island first to get them. Hopefully, if anything did go wrong, Albigard would be in a position to portal here instantaneously, and then portal straight back with the vampire cavalry in tow.

Not for the first time, it hit me exactly how heavily we were relying on our Fae ally.

"Will I be able to travel along the ley line as mist?" Leonides asked Albigard. "Because otherwise, I'm going to have to fly across on my own, so none of the Fae see me when we arrive."

"You can use the ley line in incorporeal form," Albigard told him. "There is no reason for the Unseelie to have warded the island against vampires. Most of them probably believe there is still only one in existence, and that he would have no motivation to come here."

"So is that it, then?" I asked. "Are we ready to go?"

"If you are prepared, adept," said the Fae. "Remember—you are my prisoner, your will subjugated by a more powerful being's."

I nodded, desperate to cross the last couple of hundred miles separating me from Jace. "I'm set. Let's go."

Leonides gave me a final, long look before his body dissipated into a spiraling cloud of fog. The mist curled around me like a caress, holding fast against the wind as Albigard knelt, pressing a palm to the salt-encrusted stone at our feet.

"Good luck, Vonnie!" Zorah called, as light erupted around us and jerked us away from the windswept rocks.

My first impression of Easter Island was that it was brown and green. I staggered as we appeared in a flash of light, but this time the hand keeping me upright belonged to Albigard. Cool mist brushed over my skin, the only hint that an incorporeal vampire had just slipped away into the atmosphere above us. I blinked, disoriented. Monstrous stone faces swam in my vision.

"Hold! Stay where you are!" called a voice from behind us.

I tried to whirl around to face the threat, but the fingers wrapped around my arm tightened.

"Be calm, human whelp," snapped Albigard's — *Oren's* — voice in my ear.

I dragged my emotions under control, knowing that I needed to play my role or all would be lost. Consciously, I relaxed my tense muscles and let my head hang, ignoring the prickle of awareness signifying the Fae approaching us from behind.

"Yes, Oren," I breathed.

In front of me, seven giant stone statues on a platform made of piled rocks stared past us into the distance, watching the proceedings without expression.

Albigard turned me around slowly, using the grip on my arm. I kept my gaze lowered, focused on the two pairs of boots striding toward us. Guards, I was sure.

"What is this?" demanded one of them. "We were not informed of any additional arrivals."

"Quiet!" hissed the other. "Do you not recognize a member of the Unseelie Court?" His stance shifted nervously, like he was a soldier coming to attention. "Forgive us, sir. This is highly unusual, and we were not told of your visit."

Albigard's voice dripped with Oren's disdain. "An inspection is of limited utility when those being inspected are warned ahead of time."

Despite my pounding heart, I took a moment to marvel at Albigard's pair of giant titanium balls. I had a feeling that the next couple of days were going to be a master class in lying without uttering a single untrue word.

"Of course, Your Eminence," said the guard, immediately contrite. "And... the human?"

"It was only recently located, and appears to be an unusually powerful specimen," Albigard said in a haughty tone. "As I was coming anyway, bringing it along seemed like an efficient use of resources. Now, I require transport to the city. My time is valuable, and I do not expect to be kept waiting."

"Of course, sir. Right away, sir," said the one who'd recognized Oren. "Sypho... bring a horse for His Eminence!"

Albigard stood stony and unspeaking, as unyielding as the statues at our backs. His entire being radiated impatience and implied he was surrounded by lack-wits. A few moments later, the second guard hurried up with a horse. I chanced a look at the animal, which was stout, but scruffy— remembering the mention in my research of feral horses roaming the island in large numbers.

"How far to the settlement?" Albigard demanded, taking the horse's reins.

"Four miles southwest of here, sir," said the guard. "Follow the main road, and you will find it easily. Unless you require an escort…?"

"*Hardly*," Albigard told him. The word could have cut glass. He let go of my arm and swung his body into the saddle as though he'd been doing it for centuries. Who knew? Perhaps he had been.

"Lift the human onto the saddle behind me," he commanded.

I tried not to flinch as hands closed around my waist and lifted me as though I weighed nothing. With a clumsy movement, I managed to throw my leg over the animal's back and grab Albigard around the waist to steady myself, a bit surprised when he allowed the contact without comment.

I'd been on a horse precisely twice in my life-time, and while neither instance had been particularly traumatic, they also hadn't done any-thing much to prepare me for riding four miles across country behind a disguised fairy with an at-titude.

Albigard wheeled the horse around without another word to the guards, clearly signaling that they weren't worth his time.

"Grip with your knees," he said in a low tone that sounded more like his own, once we were out of the other Fae's immediate hearing. "Keep your back and hips loose, and don't let go."

A high-pitched squeak escaped my throat as he kicked the horse into a canter. The muscles be-neath me bunched and released in a rhythmic, rolling motion that would have toppled me onto the ground in two seconds flat if not for my death grip on my companion. Wind streamed through my hair, the thud of hooves on packed dirt echoing in my ears.

Each stride jounced me violently up and down, jarring my tailbone until I tried to follow Albigard's instructions and let my hips roll with the motion. Scenery blurred past us, obscured by my watering eyes and blowing hair. But by the time I started to make out houses and other buildings breaking the monotony of grass and dirt, I was finally getting a feel for the horse's movement.

I think it was about twenty minutes or so before our surroundings changed from rural to markedly urban, with street signs and shops and houses and parks, all disconcertingly empty of life. I wasn't sure if Albigard was following some inner sense of the location of the other Unseelie, or just the signs written in Spanish. Whatever the case, he slowed the horse to a bouncy trot and wended his way through the maze of streets lined with colorfully painted houses and public art, for all the world as though he knew where he was going.

In the distance, I could hear the sound of seabirds and crashing waves.

Eventually, we ended up on a road where the buildings weren't necessarily any grander than the stores and shops had been, but were at least newer. They also had more official looking signage, with words like *Gobernacíon Provincia*, and acronyms like CONADI. This, I gathered, had been the government district of the tiny island province.

And indeed, there were now signs of life—saddled horses tied to hitching posts along the road, people entering and leaving the buildings. Or, rather... *Fae* entering and leaving the buildings. Albigard pulled up next to the place that looked the busiest, which also boasted a more modernist style of architecture than most of what we'd seen so far.

"Where are the adepts being kept?" he demanded of the first person he saw.

The Fae's eyes widened in clear recognition. "Around the corner," he said, pointing in the direction we'd just come from. "They're being housed at what was once a human sporting facility."

Again, Albigard reined the horse around without acknowledging the speaker or offering any thanks, and we were once more trotting down the road, the horse's gait jarring my already bruised seatbones. He turned left onto the first road we came to, heading toward the sound of the ocean. Houses lined the right side of the road, which was so narrow that I wondered how cars had passed each other without knocking their mirrors together. On the left side, a different kind of structure loomed ahead.

It was vastly larger than anything else I'd seen, except possibly the single 'supermercado' we'd passed on the way into town. Glass and steel formed the front wall, with sides of red brick. Beyond it lay a vast expanse of grass surrounded by netting tacked to posts, extending perhaps twenty feet above the ground. It was a sports field, as the Fae had said. Probably soccer in this part of the world, I thought.

The netting had apparently been intended to keep stray balls from flying across the roadway and into the houses on the other side, but I'd wager it was also pretty effective at keeping people from leaving easily. Because the soccer field was no longer a soccer field. Instead, it was covered by dozens of colorful circular tents, the tent-cloths dyed in jewel tones that reflected the morning light like shimmering satin.

And there were children moving among the makeshift shelters.

My breath caught, my heart forgetting how to beat for a moment. I wanted to jump off the horse... to run to the netting and peer through it, searching for messy black hair and dark, deep-set eyes. But Albigard was already guiding the animal to the main doors at the front of the stadium building, where he reined it to a halt.

"Calm," he reminded me in a tone so low that no one else would hear. "Play meek, or this will go badly for you."

I inhaled and exhaled... inhaled and exhaled, until the out-of-control feeling subsided. After a few moments, it occurred to me to focus on my pendant, as a way to regulate the wild, nervous energy flowing through me.

"I'm okay," I murmured, once I was sure it was true.

"I will leave you soon, but I will return by this time tomorrow unless I am discovered and captured," he said, in the same low tone.

"I understand."

God, I was so close now.

Albigard helped me slide down from the saddle with an elbow hooked through mine. As I hit the ground, I had to lock my knees when they wobbled after the unaccustomed time spent on horseback. He threw a leg over and stepped down neatly on the animal's other side, before leading the horse to a hitching rail and tying it next to two others.

"Come, human," he ordered harshly, back in character. Grabbing me by the arm again, he used the grip to pull me to the front doors. They opened to his touch, unlocked. Guards stood inside, and I lowered my gaze to the nondescript gray tile rather than risk meeting their eyes.

"New arrival?" one of the Fae asked blandly. There was no hint of recognition in his voice. Apparently the members of the Court were somewhat well known among the common Fae... but not universally so. It made sense, I supposed, for a race that didn't have television or even photography.

"Yes," Albigard said. "Send for your superior. I would speak with him regarding this specimen."

I suppressed a shiver at the coldness of the words, wondering for the thousandth time what sort of treatment Jace had received from the Fae since being kidnapped.

"The Overseer is otherwise engaged until midday," said the guard. "Leave the human here, and you can make an appointment to speak to him later."

"Unless he is 'engaged' with Mab herself, he will wish to speak with me now," Albigard retorted, with perfect condescension. "And unless you enjoy punishment, you will wish to inform him of my presence immediately."

The guard hesitated. "I… will inform him that his presence is requested, if that is what you wish. Stay here." He turned to leave, only to pause. "Who should I say desires a meeting?"

In a flash, I realized that Albigard couldn't answer with a lie. And if he put the guard off with some statement that it didn't matter who he was, that would decrease the chances that this 'overseer' would come.

I looked up at Albigard through my lashes, the picture of adoring meekness. "Oren? Does this man not know who you are?" I asked sweetly.

"Evidently not." The words were a foul-tempered mutter. Albigard's eyes narrowed. "Speak only when spoken to, human. No one is interested in your bleating."

In my peripheral vision, I'd seen the guard blanch an interesting shade of pale upon hearing the name. I lowered my eyes immediately, my mission accomplished.

"O-Oren of the Unseelie Court?" he stammered. "Forgive me, Your Grace! I will summon the Overseer immediately."

The guard hurried off.

"Sit," Albigard ordered me, like someone might tell a dog to sit. He gestured imperiously at a bench running along the length of the wall to our right. I slunk over without a word and sat at the end, near a dented water fountain. Focusing on my hands folded in my lap, I counted the seconds and tried not to crawl out of my skin.

It took only a few minutes for the guard to come hurrying back with — presumably — the Overseer in tow.

"*Oren*?" said the newcomer. "Good grief, how long has it been? I hardly expected you of all people to appear on my doorstep."

I tried not to tense up. That had sounded an awful lot like the greeting of a friend, or at least a friendly acquaintance. I tried to get a sense of the Overseer with my peripheral vision. He was old. Not decrepit by any stretch, but his long hair and bushy eyebrows were white, rather than any variation of the blond or copper I'd seen in other Unseelie Fae. More worrying, his face held the same cast of cruelty as Oren's, and I hoped this wasn't a case of birds of a feather flocking together.

Albigard waved the words away. "Some time, certainly. This is not a personal visit, but first I must remand this child-adept to your care. It appears to be a particularly powerful specimen, and docile, as well. Its presence should be useful to our plans."

And by 'our plans,' he sure as hell wasn't talking about the *Unseelie's* plans. I swallowed a snort at his shamelessness.

"Powerful, eh?" The Overseer gave me a shrewd once-over, and I tried to convey the sort of mindless fascination with him that I'd seen humans exhibit in Teague's presence. His head tilted with interest. "What sort of abilities does it demonstrate?"

"Elemental," Albigard said, "with particular affinities for water and air." He gestured to the water fountain. "Girl. Show the Overseer what you showed me."

While I wasn't one hundred percent sure what I was supposed to have showed 'Oren' earlier, I could guess that Albigard wanted me to do something impressive with water.

"Yes, Oren," I said eagerly. I knelt on the bench and pressed the button on the top, relieved when a stream of water arced up from the fountain. Not only would this make my little display for Oren's buddy easier, but it also meant I would be able to drink while I was here without accidentally pledging myself to another Fae.

I concentrated on the magical fields around me, hoping that my small amount of practice with Albigard in Chicago had stuck. When I could feel the flow of the water through the ether, I took a deep, centering breath, and pushed on it.

The stream of water bent from its neat arc, splattering over the edge of the fountain tray and onto the floor. I gasped, not having expected quite that much success, and the water immediately returned to its normal flow. I wasn't sure if I should grovel and apologize for getting water on the tile, or what.

Fortunately, I was saved from making the wrong decision by the Overseer's raised eyebrow and murmured, "Impressive."

Reassured, I turned my attention back to the water and unleashed a burst of hot rage at it—not difficult to conjure for the man who'd presumably been holding my son prisoner. The water sputtered and vaporized, shooting from the nozzle like steam from a leaky radiator.

"Well," the Overseer said, "that is, indeed, rather extraordinary. And you say the creature is docile?"

Albigard shrugged. "The girl seemed most agreeable when it came to the prospect of coming here."

I shot him a glance. *Hadn't I just.* He didn't acknowledge the look.

The Overseer gestured for the guard to approach. "Excellent. Creed, turn this human out with the rest. Oren, I assume you will wish to meet with the other project leaders. Come. I will arrange for refreshment, and call for them to assemble."

"Lead on," Albigard said—even as the guard, Creed, took me by the arm. Albigard followed the Overseer deeper into the building, without so much as a backward glance in my direction.

I was on my own, unless you counted a hovering vampire who couldn't materialize without trashing all our plans. Of course... Albigard was also on his own. All it would take was one personal question from Oren's old acquaintance that he couldn't answer for his cover to be blown. But I couldn't worry about him now. I had my own set of challenges.

TWENTY-FOUR

"Come, girl," Creed said stiffly. "You will be placed with the other humans. They will show you what is expected of you."

He led me toward a side door. Beyond was an echoing locker room that smelled of old sweat and mildew. We passed rows and rows of lockers—some closed, others with the doors hanging open, exposing the emptiness within. The benches had been painted blue once, but much of the paint was worn off to reveal the bare wood and metal beneath. A line of showers stood along one wall, open to the room.

We continued past them, through a room empty of everything except benches and a large dry-erase board against one wall. I guessed it had been a strategy room for the sports teams. Beyond lay another door. Unlike all the others, this one was locked. Creed took out a key and opened it, immediately locking it again behind us. We'd exited into a tunnel, and I could feel the sea breeze against my cheek. My heart hammered as Creed dragged me along the length of the dim corridor until I emerged, blinking, onto the former soccer field, now full of tents.

Excitement thrummed through me. Jace was here somewhere. He *had* to be.

"Humans!" Creed bellowed.

Several children and teens looked up from what they were doing, and hurried forward to meet us.

Creed thrust me out in front of him like I was an inanimate object he wanted to hand off to someone else as quickly as possible. "This one is new. Take care of it, and prepare it for what is required."

Apparently, that was all the introduction I was going to get, because he dropped my arm like a hot potato and stalked off, disappearing into the tunnel and, one assumed, through the locked door beyond. A selection of sarcastic quips rose to my lips, but I managed to swallow them before any could escape. I was supposed to be meek—enthralled by my captors. In truth, I had no idea what to expect from these children who'd been held under the Fae's control for weeks or months.

A girl with dull eyes and a closed-off expression stepped forward, taking charge. I thought she was probably twelve or thirteen.

"You belong to the Fae now," she said in a bored tone. "You're an adept in training, but you'll need to help with chores—cleaning, preparing food, washing clothes, that sort of thing. What did they tell you when they took you?"

There was barely any curiosity behind the question, more like she was marking it off a mental list. I wasn't sure what the answer was supposed to be, so I pulled something out of my ass that seemed plausible.

"He told me I was one of the special ones," I said earnestly. "He said I had magic, and that the

Fae would teach me how to use it. He said I could leave my old life behind."

"Everyone here is special," said the girl, still in that flat voice. "Of course, some are more special than others. Come with me. I'll find you space in a tent and get you a bedroll. Have you eaten?"

The other children had been watching silently, but once it seemed clear someone else was taking control of things, they wandered back to what they'd been doing before.

"I had breakfast already, thanks," I said, since I couldn't be sure if the food was a Fae gift.

The girl nodded.

"What's your name?" I asked.

"Elsie," she said, pointedly not asking mine in return. "Come on."

I walked with her toward the tents, and she kept shooting me little sideways glances along the way. Then she stopped abruptly. I stopped as well, turning to face her.

"What's that necklace?" she asked, startling me.

My hand flew to Mabel's pendant. "You can see it?"

Which... *yeah*. Not really the smoothest way to downplay things, now that I thought about it.

She frowned. "It's kind of, I dunno, flickering in and out. How are you doing that?"

I dropped the pendant into the collar of my t-shirt to hide it—*also* not the smoothest reaction.

"It's nothing," I tried. "A gift from my aunt. It just... uh... does that sometimes."

Christ, I was bad at this.

Elsie looked at me shrewdly. "It's magic. They're not going to let you keep it, you know."

I shrugged, feigning indifference. "It doesn't matter. It's just a stupid gift. I'll give it to the next Fae I see; I didn't know I wasn't supposed to have it."

Internally, I was running through possibilities a mile a minute. Without a mirror, I had no way of knowing if the protective warding was working or not. It was possible that Elsie could only see it because of her own magic… but that seemed kind of unlikely if Edward and Albigard had thought it would fool the Fae.

I tried to remember what Edward had said about the spell.

I put as much magical protection over it as I could, he'd told me. *Casual touch won't harm it. Sacred waters probably wouldn't do it much good, and I'd avoid getting salt on it.*

Salt. Oh, *crap.* I'd stood on Salas y Gómez, battered by sea spray. *Saltwater* spray. Had the salt damaged the sigils? Were the waters around these islands sacred? Should I ditch the necklace before a Fae saw or sensed it?

I decided not to. There didn't seem to be any Fae in the immediate area, and it seemed smarter to hold on to it as long as I could.

Elsie seemed to lose interest, thankfully. She resumed walking, and gestured toward the nearest tents. "We sleep four to a tent. Red is for girls, Blue is for boys, and purple is for genderqueer or non-binary. Girls and enbies shower in the mornings; boys shower in the evenings. There's a rota for chores in the mess tent — that's the big yellow one in the center. Oh, and don't touch the boundary nets — they're enchanted. The Fae say touching them will kill you, and no one's been dumb enough to test it."

There it was... the bars on the cage.

"I don't want to leave. I just got here. When do we learn about magic?" I asked, hoping to ease the conversation toward situations where all of the children were grouped together. I'd been scanning the surroundings for any sign of Jace, but it seemed that most of the kids were still in their tents. It was early, after all, and teenagers in particular weren't known for rising with the sun.

"There are lessons at mid-morning, early afternoon, and late afternoon," Elsie said. "Mid-morning is life-magic, and the afternoon ones are elemental magic. You have to attend all of them, but obviously you're only required to do the actual lessons for your type. Well... unless you're Mr. Special, anyway." She rolled her eyes dramatically.

"Mister... Special?" I echoed. "What do you mean?"

She waved a hand, becoming more animated. "There's a kid here who has both kinds. We call him Mr. Special because the Fae are always going on about him."

The jolt in my chest felt like I'd been struck by lightning. And that was ridiculous. Elsie might have been referring to any kid here. Yet... in that moment, I *knew*.

Richard, with his spectral life-magic wolf.

Me, with my elemental magic.

Magic among humans has nearly died out over the millennia — as the Fae intended, at least until recently, Albigard had said.

Two rare people, with two different forms of magic, randomly coming together and producing a child rarer than either of them. *Holy shit*. How could I not have known? I'd have sworn blind that Jace had never once shown magic in fourteen years…

I needed to pull myself together.

"Oh," I managed. "That kinda blows, that he's stuck doing twice the work. Could I… meet him?"

That… had not exactly been subtle.

Elsie rolled her eyes again. "God, don't tell me you're going to be another one of his groupies. I'm sure you'll see him around, but he's probably still asleep."

I wanted to ask her which tent was his. I wanted to ask *so badly*. But… there was looking like a shallow dork, and there was looking outright suspicious. I had time. I would be able to find Jace during this mid-morning lesson, when all the children were together. It would be foolish to push my luck when it wasn't necessary.

"Okay, cool," I said, and followed Elsie toward the collection of red tents.

By the time Elsie found me an empty place in a tent with two Black teenagers and an Asian girl of about six, it was time for the life-magic lesson. I had no idea what to expect, and in truth, I hardly cared as long as Jace was there.

Everyone gathered in a corner of the field that was free of tents or other obstructions. The kids sorted themselves into three groups by age, and each group faced a Fae instructor. Under other circumstances, I might've taken time to consider what it meant that Unseelie Fae—whose talents lay with elemental magic—were teaching a class on life magic rather than bringing along some Seelie Fae to do it. However, I was much more focused on the fact that I'd joined the group of teenagers, but I could still see no sign of Jace.

There were dozens of kids in each age group— maybe sixty or seventy at a guess. But I should have been able to see him...

Our Fae instructor called the class to order, only to pause, his eyes looking past us. I turned, and my heart skipped a beat as I saw a painfully familiar figure hurrying across the grass. Brown eyes... gangly body... messy cowlick of black hair falling across his forehead.

Jace was here. *I'd found my son.*

I held my breath, because I wasn't sure I could keep some sort of noise from escaping if I let it out. A sob, or a cry, or his name—

"Your unusual abilities do not give you leave for tardiness, adept," the Fae said severely.

"I know, sir—I'm sorry," Jace said sheepishly, skirting the other kids to go to the front with the handful of other children with life magic. "It won't happen again."

The Fae's lips twitched down, but he said no more about it, instead launching into a long lecture on some esoteric aspect related to controlling plants. It was probably both interesting and educational. I couldn't say for certain, since I could barely tear my eyes away from the back of Jace's head.

I suppose I was lucky that the Fae apparently didn't go in for making a big fuss about new students, preferring to simply throw newbies in the deep end and let them cope on their own merits. It was all I could do to sit still while the lesson dragged on, progressing to a practical component where each teenager who had the aptitude attempted to make a flower bud bloom.

Three of them managed it. Five didn't. Jace held his flower, staring at it in focused concentration. The petals burst open, but with too much force — sticky sap dripping down as they wilted.

The Fae snatched the ruined bloom back and held it up. "This adept mixed life and elemental magic at the same time," he said loudly, for the benefit of the whole class. "In doing so, he succeeded with neither. You must increase your discipline if you are ever to succeed." This last, to Jace.

Jace nodded, looking down, embarrassed heat rising in his cheeks. I had to clench my hands until my fingernails dug into my palms to keep from moving.

"You are dismissed," said the Fae. "You will be expected to retain this material for a test tomorrow." He waved a hand, and the teenagers began to disperse, muttering to each other.

My heart leapt. Unable to stay still any longer, I popped up from my position seated on the grass like a jack-in-the-box. Several girls and a couple of boys were clustered around Jace, apparently vying for his attention. From the glimpses I could catch through the little knot of people, he looked a bit overwhelmed and distant. This wasn't surprising. He'd always been shy — not to a debilitating degree, but I could only imagine that suddenly being the popular guy everyone wanted to talk to was freaking him out.

I wasn't doing so well with the whole subtlety thing to this point, and that wouldn't be changing in the next few minutes. Pulse thundering, I strode up to the group and squeezed through the ranks until I was face to face with my son — gloriously alive, and hopefully on the cusp of rescue.

"Hi, I'm new," I said, calling on every bit of acting ability I possessed to keep my voice and expression steady. "I can do life magic and elemental magic, and Elsie said you were the same way. Can I talk to you alone for a few minutes?"

Jace blinked at me, no recognition in his eyes... not that there should have been, obviously.

"Um, yeah. Sure," he said. "I was just going to get some lunch. Want to walk with me?"

There were some sounds of disappointment from the others, but no one made a fuss as Jace gestured toward the huge yellow tent in the middle of the field and started walking. I fell in beside him, my heart still pounding with excitement and the dangerous desire to throw my arms around him and never let go.

"So, uh… you just got here?" he asked, sneaking a glance at me.

"This morning," I said. "They took me away from my family. Kidnapped me, and brought me here."

His eyes went distant; a little glazed. He didn't reply.

I forged ahead. "But I've got a way out. There's a guy here who can get me back home. He can get you home, too. We just have to be ready when he comes for me."

Jace stopped dead, staring hard at me. "Are you being serious right now?" he asked.

I tugged his arm, pulling him out of the way of the other children filtering toward the mess tent. I'd thought about this during the lecture, and now my fingers grasped the familiar clasp of my necklace and unhooked it. From my perspective, I couldn't tell if the spell keeping it invisible was working or not—I could always see it, unless I looked in a mirror. But it was clear the wards were wearing off, and once they did, Albigard would probably be able to track it.

"Deadly serious," I told him, holding out the pendant. "Take this. If we're separated when my friend comes, he should be able to find you as long as you've got it."

He stared at my hand. "There's nothing there."

"Yes there is." I grasped his hand and lowered the necklace into his palm, closing his fingers around it. As soon as I stopped touching it, it faded from my view, invisible. "It's magic, but the invisibility spell is giving out. Once you can see it, you, uh... you might recognize it."

Jace's lips parted in surprise when he felt the solid object in his hand. He looked at his closed fingers, a furrow forming between his dark brows. His gaze lifted to me, the frown deepening. His mouth opened and closed a couple of times, like words were trying to get out, but couldn't. Then he drew in a deep breath and took a step back.

"Guards!" he cried. "Somebody get the guards!"

TWENTY-FIVE

My stomach dropped straight through the ground. "Jace, *no!*" I stumbled backward. Jace was still backing away, as well. Around us, children stopped and stared. Some of them turned and started running, calling for help. I looked around wildly, part of my mind screaming at me to run. But run where? It was a flat soccer field surrounded by a deadly magical barrier. And hiding in a tent would be pretty useless if the children could just point to it and say, 'She's in that one.'

Dear god, why hadn't it even occurred to me that this might be a possibility?

"Jace, please," I begged, hearing the quaver in my voice. "You don't mean this! Don't you want to get out of here, back to your moth—" I cut myself off. "To... your family?"

Jace watched me with haunted eyes, his chest rising and falling rapidly. He didn't reply—and then it was too late, because two Fae guards were jogging toward us.

"It's her," called a girl of about twelve, pointing at me. "She's the one!"

One of the Fae snapped out a hand with a sharp gesture. A loop of light flew toward me, wrapping around my neck and tightening with the same force as a physical noose. *Collaring me.* My fingers scrabbled at the constriction, but there was nothing there to grasp.

"What is the meaning of this?" snapped one of the guards. It wasn't Creed—not that it really mattered.

"Sh-she said she was going to escape," Jace said, the stutter that he'd left behind in grade school hitching in his voice. "She w-wanted me to come with her. Said she had a friend who would help."

He was still clutching the pendant, but to anyone else, it would look like he was simply clenching his fist.

"I see," said the guard. "Very well. You were wise to call for help, adept."

Jace didn't look as though he felt wise. He looked anguished. I tried to reach for him, but the guard snatched the magical leash he was holding and jerked me toward him.

"Get the Overseer," he told his companion. "I don't recognize this one. It must be new."

As they hauled me away, I craned to look back at Jace. He was staring at his open palm, and I could just make out a glint of red flickering in and out of existence. His eyes lifted to me in the instant before I was yanked forward, stumbling, and pulled out of sight among the tents.

———◆———

The guards brought me to a part of the sports building I hadn't seen on the way in, and left me in a bare room with no window. I tried to go to the door to test the lock once they'd gone, but the magical pressure around my neck tightened before I could get within arm's reach. I backed up a step and the pressure eased, as though I really was tied up with a collar and leash.

They returned a small eternity later, and dragged me to what had once been a conference room, done up in bland shades of brown and tan with a large, oval table dominating the space. In addition to the magic collar, I now had a loop of invisible force binding my wrists behind my back, and I was trying hard not to panic as my mind helpfully replayed flashbacks of my kidnapping by Ivan on a continuous loop.

The Overseer sat in the place of honor at the far end of the table, flanked on the left by Albigard, with half a dozen other Fae arrayed around them. The only one I recognized was the instructor from this morning. I couldn't tell if I was imagining the way Albigard's eyes seemed to say, *'Well, that certainly didn't take long to go off the rails,'* or not.

The guard shoved me forward to stand at the front of the room. "This is the human that caused the disturbance, Your Honors. One of the others claimed it was planning escape, and had inside assistance."

The Overseer scowled. "Assistance? What kind of *assistance*?"

"The other human stated that this one claimed to have a 'friend who would help.' That was the extent of the detail it provided."

The Overseer's gaze slid to Albigard, and there was suspicion in it. My heart—still battered by Jace's anguished moment of betrayal—sank.

"Oren... you arrived with this creature only this morning—proclaiming its docility in glowing terms, as I recall. Can you explain this?"

Albigard looked unconcerned—cool as the proverbial cucumber. "I cannot. Perhaps it is delusional. I agreed to transport it, and picked it up this morning after seeing a demonstration of its powers." He tilted his head, running a cold gaze over me. "It did, in fact, seem to be quite compliant—even eager."

The Overseer's expression turned calculating. "Is it possible that it was trying to make its way here for a specific purpose?"

I hid a wince. *Ouch. A little too close for comfort there, buddy.*

Another of the assembled Fae scoffed. "Surely such a plot would be beyond a creature like this. It is only a youngling."

At this point, I was beginning to wonder if they intended to address me at all, or just sit there sneering at me while they insulted my intelligence and compared me to an animal. Not that I had any good plan for defending myself, mind you. I couldn't claim Jace had been lying without turning the spotlight on him, and I doubted the 'sorry, I panicked' defense would hold much sway with this room full of dour Fae bastards.

"Something's not right," muttered one of the unfamiliar Fae.

He was an old man—older by far than the Overseer, with stooped shoulders and rheumy eyes.

"What do you mean, Master Balfour?" the Overseer asked, looking at me with fresh interest.

Balfour rose, bracing against the table. "There is Fae magic surrounding her. Well hidden, but definitely present." He gestured to the guards. "Hold her."

I tensed, but it wasn't as though I was going anywhere, bound as I was. I couldn't help flicking a quick glance at Albigard, whose disdainful 'Oren' expression seemed to have frozen somewhat unnaturally.

"Stay away from me!" I warned, knowing it was a waste of breath even as the words passed my lips.

"Quiet," said the ancient Fae, and suddenly it was difficult to look away from him. My pendant was gone... my talisman against Fae influence...

Balfour loomed in my vision, magnetic and fascinating. I wanted to please him. I wanted...

His hand rested on my forehead, his fingers splayed over my skull.

"The human is glamoured," he said. "A skillful job, too."

"Break it," The Overseer said sharply.

I stood in a fugue as Balfour closed his eyes in concentration. A moment later, a sharp chill rushed over my body, and I shuddered. Balfour backed away, his mental grip on me loosening at the same time his fingers slid away from my head. I blinked rapidly, trying to recall myself to my surroundings.

"What is the meaning of this?" the Overseer hissed, rising slowly from his chair and turning to look down at Albigard.

Albigard rose as well, looking wary.

"The Oren I know is a specialist in glamour and its detection," continued the Overseer. "The Oren *I* know would never be fooled by a human wearing a Fae's disguise. *Explain yourself.*"

Albigard lifted his chin. "I have no intention of explaining myself to you, or anyone here." The words were delivered in Oren's haughty voice, but even I could tell Albigard was losing the crowd.

This was confirmed an instant later, when the Overseer barked, "Balfour! Check this Fae for glamour."

I held my breath, but Albigard only gave the man a thin, humorless smile.

"I think not," he said, flicking a portal into existence behind him with a subtle movement of one hand.

"Stop him!" the Overseer roared.

But it was too late. He'd already stepped backward and disappeared, the flaming oval snapping shut the moment he was through it.

Shocked silence echoed around the room. Albigard hadn't even spared me a glance before casually throwing me to the lions.

The others were looking at me, though. In fact, every eye in the room was now firmly on me. I tilted my chin up and pulled my shoulders back, hoping it would help hide how hard I was trembling as I met the Overseer's gaze.

"Right, you Fae bastard," I said, channeling every ounce of maternal rage I'd been carrying around for the past several weeks into my voice. *"What the hell have you done to my son?"*

End of Book Three

Vonnie's story concludes in *Vampire Bound: Book Four.*

To discover more books by this author, visit www.rasteffan.com